'Callie Labeau?'

The woman turned and Matt was hit with a vision of hair the color of dark honey, wide brown eyes, and a slim but clearly female body filling out the bust of her gown. Appreciation thrummed through his veins, but he ignored the distracting sensation.

'Matt Paulson.' He stuck out his hand.

'Colin called and said he was sending you my way.'

A palm briefly pressed against his. The soft skin and the drawl, as honey soaked as her hair, brought to mind hot Southern nights filled with heated skin and sweat-soaked sheets.

Stick to the plan. Get in, take care of the problem, and get out.

She released his hand and her lips quirked. 'Though Colin didn't mention he was sending you *now*.'

There was no irritation in her voice, only the calm tone of one who dealt with life's surprises and upsets with grace and dignity. He liked her already.

She'd need that skill set for what he had in mind.

ONE NIGHT IN NEW ORLEANS

Check out the first book in this duet:

NO TIME LIKE MARDI GRAS
by Kimberly Lang
(February 2013)
which is also set in the city of New Orleans, Louisiana, USA!

DON'T TELL THE WEDDING PLANNER

BY
AIMEE CARSON

First published in Great Britain 2014
by Mills & Boon, an imprint of Harlequin (UK) Limited,
Eton House, 18-24 Paradise Road, Richmond, Surrey, TW9 1SR

© 2014 Aimee Carson

ISBN: 978 0 263 24240 9

The summer she turned eleven **Aimee Carson** left the children's section of the library and entered an aisle full of Mills & Boon® novels. She promptly pulled out a book, sat on the floor, and read the entire story. It has been a love affair that has lasted for over thirty years.

Despite a fantastic job working part-time as a physician in the Alaskan Bush (think *Northern Exposure* and *ER*, minus the beautiful mountains and George Clooney), she also enjoys being at home in the gorgeous Black Hills of South Dakota, riding her dirt bike with her three wonderful kids and beyond patient husband. But, whether she's at home or at work, every morning is spent creating the stories she loves so much. Her motto? Life is too short to do anything less than what you absolutely love. She counts herself lucky to have two jobs she adores, and incredibly blessed to be a part of Harlequin Mills & Boon®'s family of talented authors.

Other Modern Tempted™ titles by Aimee Carson:

THE UNEXPECTED WEDDING GUEST

This and other titles by Aimee Carson are available in eBook format from www.millsandboon.co.uk

To the man who made all this possible.
Thanks, honey. I love you.

PROLOGUE

Dear *Ex Factor,*
I'm in desperate need of help. My best friend is marrying my former boyfriend and now she's asked me to be her maid of honor. My ex and I dated for over three years and everyone thought we'd eventually marry. The breakup was messy, but when he started dating my BF we all managed to reach an understanding. I'm really happy for my girlfriend and I want to be there for her on her big day, but I dread all the comments from friends and family. What should I do?

Callie: First off, congratulations to all three of you for working through your differences so that everyone remains friends. Secondly, I've been in your shoes, having recently arranged the Ex-Man's wedding—*my* ex-boyfriend—which he ruined with a zombie invasion. :) If *you* are happy for the bride and groom then most of the guests will see this. Unfortunately, there will be those with thoughtless comments and questions. I found it best to be prepared. So formulate a few vague, generic responses beforehand so you won't get caught unprepared.

Ex-Man: I think you only need one response: "I'm mainly here for the free food and beer." And if you're planning a zombie invasion to liven up the reception, don't tell the wedding planner.

CHAPTER ONE

MAN, WHAT A lot of work just to get hitched.

Matt weaved his way through the sightseers enjoying the ballroom of the historic Riverway mansion, a plantation that had once taken part in producing 75 percent of the world's cotton, but was now reduced to group tours and a venue for weekend events. He knew he was headed for the outdoor, private wedding reception when he spotted two Southern belles in authentic dress.

Choosing a Civil *War* theme to celebrate a marriage seemed wrong. But who knows, maybe the couple enjoyed the irony? Regardless, given the authentic mansion worthy of Scarlett O'Hara and the costumes of the guests, the wedding planner was either a genius...or insane. Matt was pulling for the latter, because he absolutely needed Callie LaBeau to be insane. If she were a reasonable, rational individual, she'd refuse Matt's request. Which meant his plans to fly in, fix his problem and fly back home would be over. And he'd be screwed.

Catching up with the two ladies in 1800s dresses, petticoats rustling beneath, wasn't hard. Their hoopskirts caught as they tried to open one of the French doors leading to the backyard, and their attempt to cross the threshold side by side didn't work out so well.

Matt bit back the grin and the fatigue of thirty-six hours on two hours of sleep, pulling open the other door.

The one in an ugly yellow-colored dress tossed him an inviting smile. "Thanks."

"Bathroom breaks must be a real bitch," Matt said.

The lady in lavender laughed. "You have no idea."

"Do either of you know where I can find Callie La-Beau?" he asked.

Lavender lady jerked her thumb toward one end of the outdoor reception. "Last time I saw her, she was over by the bar."

Matt took that as good news. Alcohol would definitely be a requirement in a crazy setting such as this, hopefully softening the wedding planner toward Matt's cause.

"I think she's the only one in royal-blue." Yellow dress sounded a little jealous.

Matt took the exit leading out to the twenty-acre grounds that smelled of freshly cut grass and held the crowd of wedding guests in Civil War costumes. Kerosene lamps sat on tables covered in white and dangled alongside Spanish moss in the giant oaks. The trees provided a canopy for the reception, the soft lamps casting a glow against the twilight sky.

He hoped the lamps were fake or the theme would soon be overrun by the yellow of firemen suits.

Fortunately, the lighting was low enough that Matt's dark pants and white, button-down shirt blended with the attire of the staff posing as servants. As for the male guests, half wore blue Union uniforms while the others sported gray Confederate uniforms—given the choice of a Southern theme, most likely the bride's side of the family. Matt scanned the brightly colored Southern belle dresses dotting the scene and spied one of royal-blue in front of an old-fashioned buggy being used as a bar.

Relief relaxed his shoulders. Today's four-hour flight to New Orleans had been turbulent and hot, hopeless for snagging a few minutes of shut-eye. A cold beer would go down good about now.

He approached the makeshift bar and leaned a hip against the wagon. "Callie LaBeau?"

The woman turned, and Matt was hit with a vision of hair the color of dark honey, wide, brown eyes and a slim but clearly female body filling out the bust of her gown. Appreciation thrummed through his veins, but he ignored the distracting sensation.

"Matt Paulson." He stuck out his hand.

"Colin called and said he was sending you my way."

A palm briefly pressed against his. The soft skin and the drawl, as honey-soaked as her hair, brought to mind hot, Southern nights filled with heated skin and sweat-soaked sheets.

Stick to the plan, Paulson. Get in, take care of the problem and get out.

She released his hand and her lips quirked. "Though Colin didn't mention he was sending you *now.*"

There was no irritation in her voice, only the calm tone of one who dealt with life's surprises and upsets with grace and dignity. He liked her already.

She'd need that skill set for what he had in mind.

"Colin told me I could find you here." He scanned the guests milling about. "I assumed you were scoping out a venue for an event. He didn't mention I was walking into the middle of an actual wedding reception."

"Colin's a good friend, and I owe him a lot. But he's

an obsessed gamer," she responded with a shrug that said it all.

Matt understood. Over the course of the past two years, he'd learned that the geekdom world was built on the backs of those whose lives revolved around the game. Outside social conventions often didn't compute. His brother's life currently consisted of work and spending hours immersed in the world of *Dungeons of Zhorg,* having traded one obsession for another. Matt just hoped Tommy's current fixation lasted.

Because dungeons and dragons and trolls beat the hell out of crystal meth.

As always, the years-old ache in his chest hurt as he remembered a time when his brother was gaunt, paranoid and delusional. Sick and wasting away right in front of Matt's eyes.

His stomach roiled, and he pushed the memories aside. "Should we meet up tomorrow or do you have a minute?"

"I'll be out of town all day on Saturday. How long are you in New Orleans?"

"Until Sunday morning."

She let out a huff of humor. "Now it is, then."

Callie reached into the bodice of her gown. The sight of those graceful fingers dipping into her cleavage hiked his brow and tightened his groin. Fortunately, he kept his expression one of amused sarcasm rather than the truth: a sleep-deprived guy who found the sight a total turn-on. A grin curled her mouth as she pulled out a tiny pocket watch.

"I try to keep things as authentic as possible. As the one in charge, that makes things difficult. Working without my tablet has been a real pain." She glanced at the time and blew an escaped strand of honey-colored hair from her cheek. "My assistant can keep an eye on things for a bit. But you only have twenty minutes until I need to prepare for the cutting of the cake."

Twenty minutes wasn't a lot of time to convince someone to do the impossible.

He ordered a beer and Callie requested a club soda. After she spoke with her assistant, who wore a similar gown in red, and looked a lot more harried than the wedding planner herself, they headed to a small bar along the back of the house that wasn't in use.

"What I wouldn't give to lean back in that seat right now." Callie looked longingly at a chair at one of the few empty tables, like a student eyeing an espresso after an all-nighter. "But this dress makes relaxing impossible. And I'm tired of sitting up straight."

"That getup doesn't look comfortable, either."

"The petticoat is stiff and the corset makes breathing impossible." She leaned against the counter, her brown eyes intrigued. "So tell me about your wedding-day fantasies, Mr. Paulson."

A bark of shocked laughter shot from his mouth. Hell, before he could think about tying the knot he'd have to be in one place long enough to successfully date someone. And that wouldn't happen anytime soon. If ever.

How many times had he tried, and miserably failed, to be the long-distance boyfriend? How many times had he tried, and failed, to keep a relationship going? An occasional round of great sex was one thing, but that held a woman for only so long. And there weren't many willing to play second chair to his responsibilities to Tommy. Eventually, they all left, the resentment toward his priorities too much to overcome.

Matt cleared his throat. "I'm not here to discuss my fantasies."

Fantasies.

Another stab of awareness hit, stronger than the one before. Damn, why were they even using the word? Currently *his* fantasies consisted of a brown-eyed beauty wearing an old-fashioned dress with a ridiculous hoop beneath. But the thought of unlacing a corset was surprisingly...hot.

He settled next to her at the counter. "I'm here about my brother's wedding."

Was that a hint of interest that flickered through her eyes?

Before he could decide, she glanced down at her drink and took a sip before carefully setting down her glass. "So why isn't he here?"

"Can't get the time off work."

More accurately, with Tommy's track record, he couldn't risk losing another job.

"And the bride to be?" she drawled.

A history as bad as the groom's. Perhaps worse.

"They had prior commitments," Matt said instead, sending her a smile that didn't encourage further questioning. "I had a few days off, so I volunteered to come down and get the ball rolling."

She eyed him steadily. "Dedicated of you."

Matt's lips quirked dryly. She had no idea.

"What can I say?" he said with an easy shrug. "I'm a hell of a brother."

Matt glanced down at the woman who stood a good six inches shorter than him. A height which was just high enough for a great view down the front of that ridiculous outfit that displayed her breasts as though they were a commodity. Perhaps during the time period of the dress, they had been.

Man. He rubbed his eyes. The fatigue was clearly getting to him. He'd worked four twelve-hour shifts in a row, the E.R. packed with patients every night—just how he liked it. The last night he'd encountered a trauma case that left him flying high on adrenaline, unable to sleep. He loved the challenge, and he was damned good at emergency medicine, too. He'd finished up a satisfying two weeks of work in one of the busiest E.R.s in Los Angeles and had been set to climb on a flight back to Michigan to check on Tommy. Until his brother had called and shared his and Penny's plans for the wedding. So, instead, Matt had headed to LAX and climbed onto a plane bound for New Orleans.

"Don't be too impressed, Mr. Paulson."

Matt blinked, forcing himself back to the present and the lovely set of boobs. "Come again?"

"The corset pushes everything up. They're not as big as the dress makes them look."

He quirked an eyebrow, amused by her admission. "Who said I was looking?"

Even the laugh that escaped held a hint of the South. "No one had to say anything, Mr. Paulson. I can see your eyes with my own."

Matt scrubbed a hand down his face. "Sorry. I haven't had much sleep in the past thirty-six hours and I got a little distracted. And I think you should call me Matt." A hint of a grin finally crept up his face. "I'm guessing the formalities aren't necessary once you get caught leering down a woman's dress. How much time do I have left?"

Her lips quirked as she reached in to her bodice "It's now seven forty-five. You have ten minutes left." She tipped her head curiously. "Don't you wear a watch?"

"I do," he said. "I just enjoy the sight of you pulling that watch out of your dress."

Her warm laugh encouraged him to settle more comfortably against the counter.

"So tell me about your *brother's* wedding fantasy," she said.

She turned and leaned her elbows back on the counter, and he wondered if she knew the position put her on even better display. From the focused look on her face, he'd say no. The woman had slipped fully into themed-wedding-planner mode. He forced his eyes away from the expanse of skin of her bared shoulders and the line between the curve of her breasts.

"Simple," Matt said. "His fantasy involves a video game."

Callie groaned. "That's why Colin sent you to me."

"Tommy and Penny want their wedding to be a *Dungeons of Zhorg* weekend set here in New Orleans," he said. "And since I volunteered to come and hire someone to organize the wedding, I wanted to check and make sure there wouldn't be any legal problems with the plan. So I hunted Colin down to clear up any copyright hassles."

"Which would only be a problem if you were selling tickets to the public. I assume this is a private party."

"More or less."

Her eyebrows drifted higher. "So which is it, more or less?"

Here was where things were about to get tricky.

Matt shifted on his feet, trying to get comfortable against the counter. "They want to combine their wedding with a LARP event for their fellow gaming friends. You know, a live-action—"

"Live-action role-playing. Yes, I know. I dated Colin long enough to be well versed in geek speak."

Matt felt his brow crinkle in surprise.

So Colin was her ex. When Matt had searched the creator of *Dungeons of Zhorg* out at Rainstorm Games and found him in his office late on a Friday afternoon, Matt's opinion of the geeked-out gamer had been complete. Fortunately, the man had no problem with Tommy and Penny's plans. In fact, Colin thought a newspaper article about the event would be good publicity for his game. Matt had told him he'd check with Tommy before agreeing, but figured his brother and the equally geeked-out fiancée would be thrilled. Matt could just see the headline now.

Ex-Drug Addicts Saved by Finding True Love Through the *Dungeons of Zhorg.*

Everyone would love the story. Hell, *Matt* loved the story.

He just wished he could believe the current state of affairs would last.

The familiar surge of unease filled his stomach like a concrete truck unloading its contents. Damn. If he'd learned anything over the years of Tommy's addiction, it was that taking care of today was the best Matt could do. Sometime it was *more* than Matt could do.

And often, his best just hadn't been good enough.

Matt pushed the thought aside and returned to the more interesting topic of Callie. "You and your ex must have remained pretty good friends if he's sending you my business."

Her eyes crinkled at the corners. "You'd have to pry the game controller from his cold, dead fingers before the man would admit the truth, but he owes me. I helped him track Jamie down after they first met. Now they're married." Callie let out a chuckle. "That and he wants to ensure the wedding gets done right. You know, with the proper attention to Zhorg detail." He heard, rather than saw, the roll of her eyes in her tone. "But a ceremony shouldn't be too hard to pull off."

"Actually, the entire weekend needs to be planned."

"Wait," she said, straightening up from the counter to face him. "I thought you just needed me for the wedding part. You want me to be in charge of the entire LARPing *event?*"

After several years of experience as the locums doctor in various E.R.s located in big cities across the country, Matt had learned how to handle addicts flying higher than a kite, as dangerous as a violent criminal.

Much like a cornered wild animal, the key was to never let 'em see you flinch.

He maintained her gaze and adopted his best soothing tone. "Yes. But the weekend doesn't need to be that elaborate. Throw up a few tents, offer a little food, and the guests bring their own costumes. And we can call it a day."

He knew he'd totally downplayed Tommy and Penny's vision for the weekend, but Matt thought they were dreaming too big anyway. He'd told them both pulling off exactly what they wanted would be impossible, short of crawling into the video game itself.

Her brow scrunched and several seconds ticked by.

"How much time do I have?" she asked.

"Two months."

"You're kidding, right?"

"I'm completely serious."

"Impossible. Sorry, Mr. Paulson, you'll have to find someone else." She reached out and took his wrist, pushing up his sleeve to peek at his watch. And then gave him a pretty smile. "Time's up."

Momentarily stunned, he watched her head toward the cake table.

Until he remembered his goal, and took off, following her through the crowd. "I love what you did with *The Wizard of Oz* wedding," he said, keeping stride with Callie. "And having the Mad Hatter as the wedding officiant in the *Alice in Wonderland* theme was inspired."

Did he sound as stupid as he felt?

"How did you learn about that?" she asked.

"Colin gave me one of your brochures. He said you're the best in the business."

Callie cast him an amused glance but kept on walking. "Are you trying to use flattery to change my mind?"

"You bet," he said. "Is it working?"

"Not yet, but feel free to keep trying."

"The Elizabethan venue was spectacular—" he dodged two Southern belle dresses and a Confederate soldier "—and *The Three Musketeers* theme was cool, as well."

She shot him a wry look. "Pirates," she said. "It was a pirates theme."

"Whatever," he said. "Who else is better qualified for a *Dungeons of Zhorg* themed wedding?"

Callie stared out across the crowd of guests milling about as they enjoyed appetizers. A furrow of concentration between her brows, she appeared to be running through the idea in her head. She chewed on her cheek before swiping her lower lip with her tongue. The sight of the now damp, full mouth was putting a whammy on his libido.

Huh, if he was this easily distracted, it was well past time he sought out some female companionship. To take the edge off, so to speak. Or maybe he simply needed sleep.

"Okay. It might be doable. Crazy, mind you. But doable," she drawled, and then looked around the current scene. "After all, crazy *is* my specialty."

Matt smiled his first real smile since Tommy had shared his engagement news and Matt couldn't decide if the marriage would make conditions better…or worse.

The potential for an epic screwup was great.

Callie sent him a wide smile back. The gesture wasn't sexual, but the genuine nature lit her eyes in a way that left them sparkling, sending another bolt of heat and awareness up his spine.

Too bad his flight out was Sunday. And there was no way he could delay the trip. He'd already gone two weeks without flying back home, to the childhood house Matt had moved back into, sharing the residence with Tommy since the very first round of rehab had failed, all those years ago.

He cleared his throat. "Fantastic," he said.

Mission accomplished. Problem addressed, solution found and past time to move on. Or, as the motto went in the E.R., treat 'em and street 'em. Everything was turning out better than he'd planned. He'd even get a full night's sleep tonight.

"Let me know how much to put down as a deposit.

I'll get you my email so you can send me the invoices as we go." He slipped his wallet from his pocket and pulled out his card, filling in the contacts. "And here are Tommy and my cell phone numbers too, just in case you have any questions—"

"Wait." Her brown eyes grew even wider as she took his card. "You're not leaving, are you?"

Concern edged up his back, making his shoulders feel stiff. "I have a hot date with the king-size bed in my hotel room—a rendezvous I'm really looking forward to. And Sunday I *have* to head back home."

Callie leaned closer, bringing that lovely view in a more direct line of vision. "Listen, Mr. Paulson."

How was he supposed to listen, much less concentrate, with a view like that? And clearly the stress of the upcoming event had knocked them back to a last-name basis instead of first.

"You're lucky I have a light enough schedule and an assistant to help me," Callie said. "But I can't do this alone. There are too many decisions that need to be made, and made quickly, too. I won't take responsibility for making the wrong ones. Someone needs to be around to help."

"Both me and my brother will be available by phone and internet."

"Not good enough. We can't afford to play phone tag. Not with so little time and so many big choices to be made."

"What choices?"

"Venue, for one. This won't be your average setting. We'll need a large outdoor park with adequate parking. Food, for another. A menu based on medieval times? Complicated. And from what I remember about LARP, there are games revolving around the video. And they'll need to be authentic."

"Tommy and Penny won't care about the details," he lied.

They would care. In fact, they'd care too much. That's what made a fan crazy enough to base their entire wedding around a video game. An obsession about even the minutest of details.

"I once had a client who said she didn't care. But she did," Callie said. "Despite the fact the bride and groom were thrilled with my work, the one paying the bills wasn't." She tipped her head. "Who's paying for all of this?"

"Me."

Something flashed in her eyes that he didn't recognize. Probably questions and comments and opinions about a wedding being paid for by the brother of the groom. Not your traditional arrangement. But then again, who else was there? No one.

And there hadn't been for a long time.

Callie, to her credit, didn't pry. "Then, officially, you'd be my boss. If you want me to agree to plan this event, you're going to have to at least stick around long enough to make a few of the major decisions."

"How long?"

"Depends on how our hunt for a venue goes. Can't say for sure. Maybe a week?"

Damn. That would mean he'd go almost a month without physically checking in on Tommy. The last time Matt had done that, he'd missed some early clues, and Tommy had wound up in rehab again.

But that was two years ago and he'd promised Tommy he'd take care of this.

Matt turned his options over in his head. As far as he could see, he didn't have any. He'd only just convinced the woman to take this project on. Refusing her now would be counterproductive. And finding someone else to participate in this harebrained idea would be absolutely impossible.

"All right," he said, raking a frustrated hand through his hair. "I'll give you until Tuesday and then we can reassess from there."

"Fine. But we need to get started right away, beginning with a meeting to list exactly what y'all want. I have to go out of town tomorrow, family stuff I have to take care of. But I'll put together a list of potential park sites and Sunday we can make the rounds to check them out. We can use the drive to put together our ideas for the wedding weekend."

Sticking around to help nail down the details for this crazy event? Not exactly what he'd had in mind when he'd climbed on the plane today. Matt could afford two more days in New Orleans before heading home. And Callie's brilliant smile helped ease the frustrating turn of events.

"Sunday morning it is," he said.

"Forecast calls for a heat wave the next few days or so." Callie's grin grew bigger. "Hope you like the weather hot, Mr. Paulson."

The playful grin brought about one of his own.

"Ms. LaBeau," Matt said, leaning close. "I like everything hot."

Matt entered his hotel room and toed off his shoes, unbuttoning his shirt as he headed toward the bathroom. Fatigue made his movement clumsy as he flicked open the front of his pants. After tossing his clothes aside, he flipped on the water and stepped inside the marble shower, groaning as hot water coursed over his hair and down his skin.

The ache in his muscles had started during the cramped four-hour flight, and now finally eased. Matt leaned his hand against the wall and bowed his head, letting the wet heat wash away the remainder of the stress of the past thirty-six hours.

It looked like his plans to get in and out of New Orleans quickly so he could check on Tommy had just bitten the dust. As a consolation, he now had a little more time to spend with Callie LaBeau. And the next time they saw each other, he will have had a full night's sleep.

As far as screwed-up plans went, this one could have been worse.

But the time had come to rethink his approach.

First up, place a call to Tommy. A phone check never gave as much information as a face-to-face interaction, but it beat no contact at all. Unfortunately, no one could assess weight loss and skin color over the phone. Of course, the first sign Tommy was slipping was the way he refused to look Matt in the eyes.

Second, the trip around town to locate an available park. Matt ignored the tightening in his groin as he considered a day in the car. With Callie. Alone. Awareness definitely hung in the air around them, though he sensed a hint of reluctance on her part. A reluctance that could have meant anything.

Because they were working together.

Because she had a boyfriend, though Matt doubted that to be the case.

Because she still carried a torch for Colin…

Matt soaped himself clean, picturing the golden skin and the honey-colored hair and big brown eyes. The little dip in her upper lip. The way she nibbled on the inside of her cheek while lost in thought. The pink tongue that licked the corner of her wide mouth.

He pictured that mouth on his skin. The teeth. The *tongue* traveling down his chest. Past his abdomen. The lips closing around his—

He slammed his eyes shut.

Fifteen minutes later, clean and refreshed and a whole lot more relaxed, Matt padded from the bathroom and into his bedroom. He dried his hair and wrapped the towel around his waist, heading to the window and pulling back the curtain. The lights of New Orleans spread out before him. As much as he dreaded the conversation, he picked up his cell phone and punched speed dial.

He hated the way his stomach tightened before every contact. After two years of a sober Tommy, Matt should have stopped bracing for the worst every time. Only problem was, Tommy had achieved sobriety before. Six times total. Every relapse had gotten harder than the one before. And had broken Matt's heart a little more.

"Hello?"

Despite everything, as always his brother's voice made Matt smile.

"Tommy. Fought any good dragons lately?"

The laugh on the other end sounded robust, easing a little of Matt's nerves.

"Dude, you should have seen the troll that Penny took down the other day," Tommy said.

"Big?"

"Massive."

"Hope her cooking isn't going to your waist. Your chain mail still fit?"

When Tommy's chuckle finally died down, he said, "That headhunter called again today."

The news formed a knot in Matt's chest and expanded, the pressure creating a wound that would never fully heal. The first time the recruiter from Jaris Hawking Healthcare had called about a job, Matt had been thrilled. At the time he'd been too busy cleaning up the last of his brother's latest mess to search for a job, but things with Tommy had seemed to be settled and Matt was ready to finally make the longed-for career move. Matt had spent hours researching the busy hospital in Miami, looking forward to the excitement he craved. But just when he'd been set to sign the papers, Tommy had relapsed again, requiring another round of rehab. And a family member to be there to ensure it happened. Matt had finally realized that he'd never be able to move.

Giving up that dream had hurt like hell, but there was no sense rehashing old disappointments.

Tommy went on, "They said they were desperate for someone with your talents."

"I hope you told him I'm still not interested." If he repeated the lie enough, he just might begin to believe it. Besides, he had more important things to ask. "How's work?" He aimed for a nonchalant tone, but he knew Tommy saw straight through the question.

"You don't need to check up on me, Matt." Tommy didn't sound annoyed, just resigned. "Work is fine. Penny is fine. *I'm* fine."

"You sure you two geeked-out lovebirds want to get

hitched during a lame-ass reenactment of a video game? Not too late to go for the Elvis wedding in Vegas. Or better yet, a pirate-themed adventure wedding in Hawaii. Think of it. A week's vacation in Maui with all expenses paid by yours truly. What better wedding gift could a brother ask for, huh? I could do with a base tan myself."

"The wedding absolutely has to be in New Orleans. We want trolls. And dragons. And Matt…?"

Matt dropped onto the bed, leaning back against the headboard and propping up his feet. "Yeah, sport?"

"I'll pay you back."

Matt's lips twisted wryly as affection kicked him the chest. Every goddamned time. The kid had spent the past twenty-five years worming his way into Matt's heart, until Tommy was so firmly entrenched, there was nothing Matt could do. He could picture his brother's wavy brown hair, earnest face and appreciative gaze. Beneath those ribs beat a heart of gold.

Amazing what havoc an addiction could inflict.

"You bet you'll pay me back," Matt said with a teasing tone. "With twenty percent interest. Wait, I forgot about inflation. Make that thirty percent. Didn't I tell you? You're my retirement fund."

"Which means you're screwed, bro."

Matt let out a scoff. "Better odds than on Wall Street."

Tommy laughed. When his brother finally grew silent, Matt went on.

"Seriously, though?" Matt said. "Don't worry about the money. That's what brothers are for. Just…"

Keep it together.
Stay clean.
Don't break my heart again.

"Just make sure that future wife of yours doesn't kick your ass on level ten like last month or I'll have to disown you," Matt said.

Matt could hear the smile in Tommy's voice. "You got it."

CHAPTER TWO

TWO DAYS LATER Callie studied Matt as he drove her Toyota out of New Orleans. It had been a long time since Callie had been so curious about a guy. Matt was friendly, charming, and sexy enough to eat with her fingers. There'd been no sign of embarrassment at being caught staring at her cleavage.

Even now the memory left her body vibrating with energy.

But a lingering hint of hesitation clung to him, a reserve that was fascinating. Intriguing. He'd shown up at the reception two nights ago with *goal* written all over his face.

They'd been traveling for about an hour now, but hadn't had a chance to talk much about business. Callie had been too busy directing him around town to potential parks to use as the site for the *Dungeons of Zhorg* weekend. The first two were mostly a bust. But she had high hopes for the one they were heading to now.

She'd asked Matt to drive, explaining she needed to take notes while they discussed the plans for the event, listing out the pros and cons of the two sites they'd just checked out. But the excuse sounded lame, even to her. Especially considering she spent half her time giving

Matt directions. But she didn't care. Because with his attention on the traffic, and her vantage point from the passenger seat, she was free to enjoy the view.

And she wasn't talking about the city she loved.

Matt's lean, muscular frame filled the driver's seat of her car. Given the heat wave that had settled in yesterday, he'd wisely chosen to wear shorts. Shorts that allowed a view of hard thighs. Muscular calves.

He'd had to push the seat all the way back to allow room for his long legs. His olive-colored T-shirt clung to a broad set of shoulders and biceps that flexed with every turn of the steering wheel. Not grossly big. More like well-defined and…just right. Enticing. Callie preferred the casual clothes to Friday night's slacks and button-down. Because today he looked more relaxed. He also looked as though he'd gotten some sleep.

A large truck ahead of them whipped into their lane, and Matt reacted instantly to avoid the hit. No cursing. No frazzled look. Not even an indrawn breath or a frown for the dangerous driver.

Just like Friday night, when he'd shown up so focused, he employed a plan-and-attack mantra while driving. *Goal* written all over his face. Focused. Decisive. He never hesitated. And he had lightning-fast reflexes, if the maneuver he just pulled was anything to go by. They turned into the parking lot of their next potential venue, a grassy park on the outskirts of town.

Matt turned off the car and glanced at Callie, and she realized he'd just caught her studying him. Very closely. And thoroughly.

"Is this the equivalent of me staring down your cleavage?" he asked.

She ignored the heat thrumming through her veins

and exited the car, missing the air-conditioning already and waiting for him to follow suit to respond. "Just admiring your quick reflexes."

From across the roof of her Toyota, his lips quirked. "So you were checking out my...skills."

She bit back a smile. "We have a lot of planning to do, Mr. Paulson."

"Matt."

"Matt," she said without missing a beat. "I'm just trying to figure you out. And decide whether you're gonna be the guy who makes my job easier or harder."

Normally she meant the words in the sense of a client being difficult. Hard to please. And far too demanding in their wedding-day wishes. Or incapable of making up their mind.

With Matt she knew the decisions would come quickly and decisively. Yep, with Matt the easier or harder delineation was based on Callie's ability, or inability, to stay focused with such a fine specimen of male anatomy on display.

"What have you decided?" he asked.

"I'm not sure yet," she said with a tiny grin. "I'll let you know when I figure it out."

After a few beats filled with a scorching temperature courtesy of New Orleans's latest heat wave and Matt's assessing gaze, he gave a sharp nod and headed up the brick walkway.

Fortunately the path was lined with oaks providing shade from the relentless sun. The playground to their left hummed with the activity of a few families crazy enough to brave the temperatures. An ice-cream truck was parked along the curb. The beautifully maintained park was clearly well run, the amenities nice. Even the current weather had been addressed. Misting machines with large fans had been set up along the path in front, providing blessed relief from the heat.

A drop of sweat trickled between her breasts and she ignored the long, lean legs of Matt as he walked beside her. The view wasn't helping her struggles with heat stroke.

"So there's a large private area of the park that is available for rent on the dates we need," she said. "This place is a little farther out of town than I wanted, but there's ample parking." She could feel his eyes on her, but she kept her focus forward as she came to a stop at the field.

She pointed at the outdoor building sitting in the middle of the field. "The pavilion can be used as the main structure and where the food will be served. We're going to want the restrooms close by, even if it does ruin the medieval feel."

"Better to ruin the Middle Ages feel than contract cholera."

Callie smiled but continued on, "There's more than enough space to set up the tents and the sites for the various games." She studied the grassy field, a natural border provided by oak trees. "We can set up the gaming tent over here."

He shot her another appreciative glance, and this time she couldn't resist.

"What?" she said.

"You've already given this a lot of thought."

"We don't have much time."

Matt leaned back against the oak. "Why did you agree to arrange this event?"

"It's my job. This is what I do."

He hesitated and crossed his arms as if settling in to wait for a better reason. Callie longed for a cool breeze, or heck, just a breeze would do. Anything to lower the temperature brought about by the Southern climate and Matt's disturbing eyes.

"Because I owe Colin," she said. "Our breakup was… complicated."

Translation: I screwed up big-time.

"But we've managed to remain friends," she went on. "And he's a regular contributor to my blog, *The Ex Factor.*"

At his look of confusion, a grin slid up her face. "It's a he-said, she-said column where readers can pose questions and we offer opinions from our unique perspectives."

"Is that the only reason you agreed to take this on? Because your ex helps you out?"

"Isn't that enough?"

He squinted across the field. "I'm sure you have better ways to spend your time than arranging a weekend LARP event."

Was he speaking for her or for himself?

Callie nibbled on her lower lip and looked across the field. How to explain? Because if her business became successful enough, everyone would forget about her mistake in college? Because maybe, just maybe, if she landed a big enough event with the proper publicity, her parents would stop waiting for her to muck up again?

She liked her life, damn it. And while she hadn't left for college with the plan of losing her scholarship and getting kicked out, she was delighted with what she'd built. She was happy, *proud* of all she'd accomplished despite her initial flub.

Now if she could only convince her family to be proud, too....

She pushed the thought away and shrugged. "Every little bit of publicity is good for business."

Matt studied her with those observant brown eyes that always set her on edge, mostly in a good way. Making her aware of what she wore. Making her aware of what she said. Normally she focused on business or was totally relaxed. Then again, her clients usually consisted of happy couples or middle-aged parents. Dreamy *eligible* men didn't knock on her doors wanting her services. And it was a little disturbing to be second-guessing every little thing as she went.

And if he thought her answer to his question was bull, he didn't say.

When she couldn't take those eyes studying her anymore, she turned her attention back to the field before them. "It's more than we need, but I think this works perfectly. You agree?"

"You're the expert."

"I'm sure I'll have to remind you of that sometime in the future." She lifted her hair from her neck, longing for a cool breeze. "Let's head back before you're treating me for heat stroke."

The walk back toward the car was even more uncomfortable, the sun now higher in the sky. Matt's silence and his occasional glances left her thinking he planned to quiz her further. And with the hot temperature, and the hotter gaze—not to mention the zillion questions she saw in his eyes—didn't make for a comfortable walk. Perhaps she should do a little quizzing of her own.

"So, tell me why you got elected to travel to New Orleans to arrange a wedding," she said.

His lips twisted wryly, but he didn't answer right away, so she went on.

"Over the years, I've worked with mothers, fathers, sisters and friends of the bride," she said. "But I've never worked with the brother of the groom before."

An amused light appeared in his eyes. "It's an honor to be your first."

She kept her gaze on his profile as they headed up the walk, the sound of the misting fans droning ahead. "Which doesn't answer my question."

"I told you, Tommy and Penny are up in Michigan. They both have jobs they can't afford to lose. And I happen to have the time."

"Where are your parents?"

"Dead."

A pang of sympathy hit, and she studied his expression, looking for clues to his thoughts. There weren't any.

"I'm sorry," she said. "How old were you?"

"Twenty-one. The year Tommy turned sixteen."

Leaving you in charge, she didn't say. Raising a teenager when Matt was barely past the stage himself had to have been a massive struggle.

Turning the news over in her head, Callie headed for one of the few massive fans that didn't have kids hopping up and down in front of it. A large oak provided shade and when she stepped closer to the machine, the cool mist hit her skin, and Callie almost groaned in relief. A fine spray of water coated her face, her neck, and her T-shirt and shorts. But she didn't care.

With the way Matt looked at her, a hosing off wouldn't be out of order.

"Where are Penny's parents?" she asked.

"They disowned her four years ago."

Disowned? Her eyebrows shot higher, but Callie held her tongue, despite the curiosity. What kind of parent abandoned their kid?

When she didn't respond, the buzz of the huge fan filled the air, and Matt shot her a look. "She's a recovering drug addict."

No wonder. The news explained the edge she sensed churning just beneath the surface of one Mr. Matt Paulson.

"That must be hard on your brother," she said.

Matt turned and faced the fan, closing his eyes and letting the mist hit his face. "He's a recovering addict, too."

She lingered on his profile as the words and everything he *hadn't* said settled deep. So much tension. So much emotion. She couldn't read the thoughts in his expression but they were present in the taut shoulders, the flat line of his mouth. His short, sandy hair grew damp and curled at the edges, just above his ears. His bangs, thicker than the rest of his hair, developed a wave as water accumulated. The drops left a sheen to his skin, his throat and those lovely, lovely arms.

Matt definitely had the sexy shtick down pat. A wet Matt? Even more so.

"Sad that Penny's parents won't forgive her," she said.

"They have their reasons." Matt didn't open his eyes, just continued to enjoy the cooling mist. Or pretended, anyway. "She put them through a lot. Lying. Stealing. Disappearing for weeks on end until they weren't sure if she was alive or dead from an overdose. I'm sure they just couldn't take it anymore. They're just trying to protect themselves."

Had Matt tried to protect himself?

"But still…" she said. She knew what it was like to screw up. Not in as grand a fashion as a drug addiction. Her screwup was tiny in comparison. But she knew how it felt to work hard to overcome your mistakes, only to have nobody let you forget.

"Now she's clean," she said.

"She's been clean before."

Callie let out a scoff. "'My good opinion once lost is lost forever.'"

He opened his eyes, and that brown gaze landed on hers, sending a self-conscious flush up her face. She could read the question and surprise in his expression. She hadn't meant to wear her own struggles quite so clearly, or to sound quite so personally invested.

She shrugged, trying to ease her discomfort. "Just a quote from Mr. Darcy, from *Pride and Prejudice*." When he didn't comment, she went on, "My favorite book."

On her thirteenth birthday her mother had taken her to the library and she'd checked out the paperback. She'd spent the next two days glued to the book, her mother practically dragging her from her room to come eat dinner. Growing up poor meant Callie could relate to the Bennet sisters. She'd admired Lizzy's courage and her determination to marry for love only, despite the very real risk of poverty, causing Callie's transformation from a total tomboy into a romantic. The book had had such an impact, she'd spent the weeks after imaging Lizzy and Darcy's wedding, and she'd developed a passion for bridal magazines and picturing the perfect ceremony.

Starting Fantasy Weddings had been a natural extension of that passion.

"I've never read *Pride and Prejudice*," Matt said.

"I'm not surprised."

A lull in the conversation followed, and she wanted to ask about Matt's experiences with his brother, to learn the details about the current state of the relationship between the two. However, Callie sensed asking anything more would go over like a hot toddy during a heat wave.

"How did Tommy and Penny meet?" she asked.

"As total geekster gamers and pros at your ex's zombie apocalypse game, they were selected as beta testers for *Dungeons of Zhorg.* That was how they met online. And then they discovered they'd fought the same addiction, and eventually fell in love. I think—" He pursed his lips. "I think the game helped keep them from slipping. Gave them something to focus on."

Which would explain Matt's willingness to take on this crazy task.

"I have to admit," she said softly, "I'm a sucker for a romantic story." And this one really struck a chord. Two people who'd lost themselves in a dark world and managed to pull out with the help of each other and a video game. Slaying dragons online as they fought their personal demons.

Callie smiled at the ridiculously fanciful thought. But no wonder Colin agreed to the weekend wedding/festival named after his latest game.

When Matt didn't comment, Callie went on, "Who's going to give Penny away?"

"She asked me, but I told her to get one of her *Dungeon of Zhorg* buddies. I can't do it because I'm Tommy's best man."

She let out an amused huff. "It's not like this is a traditional wedding. No reason why you can't be both."

"I'm not her family."

"You will be."

Two seconds ticked by before he hiked a brow. Mist had accumulated on his neck and trickled down to gather in the hollow at his throat. She had the sudden urge to lick the spot, and heat shot up her limbs and settled between her legs.

Shoot. Admiring the man was one thing. Wanting to treat him like her favorite brand of ice-cream cone was another.

And while he looked slightly put out by her pushing, the light in his eyes held a hint of amusement. "Does the family counseling come with the cost of your services or will that be extra?"

Callie grinned. "Just the cost of a trip to the ice-cream truck."

If she couldn't lick the real thing, she could at least enjoy the substitute. The lopsided smile he sent her did nothing to quell her appreciation of his form.

"So I'm buying?" he asked.

"You're buying."

In the end Callie chose a lemon-lime Popsicle, while Matt went with his favorite, chocolate. Cooler now that they were damp from head to toe, they wandered beneath the oaks back to Callie's car, in no particular hurry. Not only because of the relief they'd accomplished the most pressing task, selecting a site for the

DoZ weekend. But also because Matt felt no sense of urgency to leave.

Especially when Callie looked as if she'd just entered a wet T-shirt contest. It had been a while since his college buddies had dragged him to such an event during his relatively carefree undergraduate days. At the time he'd thought the rigors of academics and obtaining the grades for medical school had been stressful.

But then his parents had died, leaving him solely responsible for Tommy.

And the sight of Callie's lovely chest beneath the wet garments did more than just bring back great memories of happier times, it also turned him the hell on.

Not exactly conducive to his get-in and get-out goals.

Her damp shirt clung to her skin, and he could make out the lace of the bra beneath. White, if he wasn't mistaken. And if he tried hard enough, he could imagine the darker circle of skin beneath the center of each breast. He could definitely make out the rounder buds.

"I told you they weren't as big as the slutty Scarlett O'Hara dress suggested."

Busted.

The relaxed look on her face eased the tension in his shoulders. Though she certainly had good reason, she didn't appear overly annoyed by his tendency to check out her form. In fact, she seemed more...amused. As though he was just a stupid kid who couldn't help himself.

Which wasn't too far from the truth, aside from the *kid* part. The *stupid* description fit just fine.

"I promise," he said. "I'm not a total pervert."

"Does that mean you're a partial one?"

He threw back his head and laughed. When the

amusement finally passed, he shot her a grin. "I guess it's up to you to let me know."

They reached her car and Matt opened the door for her before rounding and climbing into the driver's seat.

He closed the door and faced Callie, who was still licking the Popsicle.

Why hadn't he noticed how hot the image was until now? The tip of her tongue catching the drips. The way she nibbled at the side. How much the vision reminded him of his fantasies during the jerk-off session in the shower that first night. Probably because he'd been too distracted by the sight of her breasts beneath that wet shirt.

Maybe he really was a perv.

He gripped the steering wheel. "Where to now?"

"Home," she said.

A completely inappropriate surge of adrenaline shot through his body, only to be doused by her next statement.

"I have some things I need to do today for another event coming up in two weeks," she said. "And I really want to take a shower and wash off all of this sweat. Where do you want to meet tonight to discuss the rest of our plans?"

She twisted in the seat to face him, one long *bare* calf curling beneath her. The tanned leg looked smooth and he wondered if the skin was as silky as it looked. Heat gathered at the nape of his neck, and the relentless sun through the window lit Callie's form, making ignoring her impossible.

He cleared his throat. "Preferably somewhere cool."

Her eyes lit, and that wide grin returned to her pretty face. "I have just the place."

CHAPTER THREE

CHRIST, THIS WASN'T really what he'd had in mind.

The chill seemed to hang in the air of The Frozen South, an ice bar taking up the top floor of The River's Edge Resort and Casino overlooking downtown New Orleans. The crowd fairly thick, the noise seemed even thicker. Most likely everyone else had the same idea: escape the heat wave outside. And the establishment was the perfect choice.

Ice blocks holding tiny neon lights made up the bar. Ice sofas, ice chairs and ice sculptures were the mainstay of the furniture and the décor. Fortunately, fur rugs lined the seats. Good thing, too. Anyone bold enough to drink too much in this environment might forget to protect their skin and wind up stuck to their chair. Some of the patrons chose to have their drinks served in ice cups. And because the management clearly had a sense of humor, costumers could even keep their cups. Of course, with the hot weather still chugging along outside with a relative heat index nearing one hundred degrees, by the time the club goer arrived home all they'd have is a wet hand that smelled of vodka.

But Matt's beef with the choice wasn't the crowd. Nor was it the cool temperature, a relief after the blistering day outside. Callie's frozen margarita looked inviting and his beer was the perfect temperature.

No, Matt hated the need for Callie to be covered in so many clothes.

Matt had sprung for the best cover package, which included a parka best suited for exploring the Arctic and a hat that framed her face, limiting his view of the honey hair he enjoyed. The only thing he had going for him was that she hadn't zipped the jacket closed.

He leaned in to speak at her ear. "You sure you don't want to go somewhere quieter?"

She turned to look at him. A maneuver that brought them face-to-face, her lips close to his.

Huh. The impulse to lean in and kiss Callie smacked him across the face like a pheromone-soaked glove, but he squelched the urge. How the hell could he plan this crazy wedding and get home to check up on Tommy if he was constantly looking at Callie, wondering what she'd taste like? With that honey hair and that honey accent, would her mouth have the same flavor?

A stupid, fanciful thought that was getting him nowhere closer to his goals.

He cleared his throat. "We might accomplish more without the noise."

Two beats passed, but Matt couldn't read the look in Callie's eyes.

"It feels good in here," she said. "Besides, the view is awesome."

Matt mentally shook his head and forced his gaze out the large window.

True, the lights of downtown New Orleans at night were definitely awesome. Unfortunately, he hadn't traveled to New Orleans to enjoy the view. But Callie in a blouse, wearing a sweater zipped up to her throat, paled in comparison to her breasts on display in a slutty Scarlett O'Hara dress. Or a wet T-shirt.

Though the gently curved hips and the shapely butt in formfitting jeans almost made up for the lack of cleavage.

Almost.

"So…" Callie stared down at her notebook, obviously completely unaware of the distracting thoughts mucking up Matt's concentration. "The games we've got listed so far are an ax-throwing competition, an archery competition and sword fighting. Though having all three feels redundant. Today I made a few calls and found a magician available those two days."

Magicians. Great. But Matt was too caught up by the play of beautiful lips and teeth and tongue as Callie spoke to pay much attention.

"A local group can provide something resembling strolling minstrels," Callie went on. "Though they won't be quite as authentic as we'd like. I checked with the park this afternoon, and horses are allowed. Which is good because apparently Penny would love to have jousters, so I contacted a branch of the Society for Creative Anachronism and—"

"Wait. *What?*"

Matt's mind stuck, spinning on all the information. Though only one piece of news stuck out.

Callie set her list down and looked at him. "The society is a living history group that's devoted to re-creating the Middle Ages. There's a branch just outside of—"

"No." Matt shook his head. "You spoke to Penny?"

For some reason the news felt odd. Strange.

She tipped her head curiously. "You gave me the

contact numbers, remember? So I called and spoke to both Tommy and Penny today." She hiked an eyebrow. "After all, I *am* arranging their wedding."

Matt couldn't speak, and Callie went on.

"Anyway, Tommy is gathering volunteers among their DoZ friends attending to run the sign-up for the competitions and then the competitions themselves during the event. And Penny is going to coordinate any of the Society of Anachronism volunteers who can attend on such short notice."

"Damn." Matt plowed a hand through his hair. "This thing is growing out of control."

At this rate he'd never get back home to check on Tommy. Matt's stomach tensed. It had been *how* many days since he'd last laid eyes on Tommy?

Regardless, if the explosion of the wedding weekend kept up, Matt would be stuck in New Orleans figuring out how to clean up horse dung from a park and how to find swords and— *Jesus,* why did Callie have to smell so good?

"I suppose now wouldn't be the time to tell you about the dragon Colin is donating to the cause?"

Matt rubbed his forehead. "Dragon?"

Callie's lips twisted wryly. "Not a real one, of course. One they used at the launch party of *Dungeons of Zhorg.*" She eyed him closely, like he looked as if his head bordered on exploding.

Matt wasn't sure but it might have been true.

"At least all of Tommy and Penny's guests are DoZ friends who are bringing their own costumes. Looks like you and I are the only ones who need to rent something."

Matt blinked, biting back the urge to call the whole damn thing off. "I am not dressing up as a troll."

Callie laughed. "I pictured you dressed more as a crusader. You know, chain mail and the whole nine yards. Anyway, because of Mardi Gras, New Orleans has great costume shops. I have several we can visit tomorrow."

Chain mail?

A crusader?

Christ, he'd almost rather go as a troll. The only thing he had left to hope for was finding Callie a slutty medieval gown.

"How does the dress fit?" Matt called through the dressing-room door.

"Give me a minute. I have to find my way inside the stupid thing before I can tell you. If you don't hear from me in ten minutes, send help." Callie stared down at the mound of fabric big enough to hide a nest of baby gators and their mama in. "Make that fifteen."

In truth, she needed a few minutes alone to recover.

Last night's graphic dream involving Matt made looking him in the eye this morning pretty gosh darn difficult. Colin's plans for publicity were growing and, as the publicity plan grew, so did the importance of this event. Now there was the potential of the story getting picked up by a local channel, so she did *not* need to be getting sidetracked by the killer hot looks of the brother of the groom. Still, looking hardly hurt anything…

Until the looking did indecent things to her dreams.

Callie pushed the thought aside and searched for the bottom of the dress. Actually, the outfit consisted of two pieces, the first part white satinlike material with a beautiful gold brocade pattern on the skirt. The second part was an overdress of robin's-egg-blue with a solid gold band at the bodice and split in front, forming an inverted V to showcase the design of the skirt beneath.

She slipped the first part over her head, wondering how Matt was faring with the costume-shop owner, an eccentric elderly man Callie had instantly adored.

Callie hadn't had an occasion to use this establishment before, but the moment she entered she'd known she'd found a gem of a resource. Not only did the owner carry a wide variety of quality costumes, he had a serious collection of props. And the stuff wasn't cheap and flimsy, either, but high-quality.

The huge crucifix on the shelf would be perfect for the *Interview with the Vampire* wedding she was organizing. Callie longed to come back and comb through the assortment of odds and ends, though the process would take some time. The owner was sweet, eccentric and carried a wide assortment of interesting items. Unfortunately, his organizational skills sucked. Searching through the racks and racks of costumes would have been easier if the shop was organized better. But their high-quality costumes made up for the inconvenience.

Matt probably would argue no.

A sharp knock on the door pulled her out of her thoughts. "Need help?"

She bit her lip and stared in the mirror. Handling the complicated fastening system in the back would be impossible on her own. Then again, having Matt in here, alone with her. Her back so exposed...

Say no. Tell him to go away.

"Sure," she said instead, opening the door.

In a medieval costume that would do a knight proud,

Matt stepped inside. And there wasn't a woman alive that wouldn't have been satisfied by the way his gaze landed on her figure and his eyebrows shot higher.

He let out a low whistle. "That gown is something. You look gorgeous."

A flush of heat left her feeling stupid.

Come on, Callie. Get your act together.

"Thank you," she said. "You, uh, look good, too."

Matt's pants looked appropriately made of unrefined material. Over the crudely cut, long-sleeved shirt, he wore a chain-mail shirt. A huge sword hung on the scabbard at his waist.

Matt let out a scoff. "Maybe, but this stuff is heavy."

"Most authentic costumes in New Orleans."

"I think I'd rather go with the cheap stuff that doesn't weigh a thousand pounds." He rolled those broad shoulders. "Man, how did men fight in this getup anyway?"

"I have no idea. But at least you don't have to wear a dress that pinches your waist to nothing and flattens your boobs," she said dryly.

Matt was clearly biting back a grin. "I definitely prefer the slutty Scarlett O'Hara over the prim and proper medieval princess. Allow me?" He nodded down at the laces hanging open in the back.

She hesitated a second. Was that amusement flickering through his eyes? Gritting her teeth with determination, she then turned to face the mirror. Matt stepped closer, bringing a scent of spicy soap. When she briefly met his gaze in the reflection, a shock of awareness jolted her limbs and burned her belly.

The intimacy of the room, the muted lighting and the strange costumes made the whole situation surreal and, God save her from her overactive imagination, a little romantic.

Given this was Matt in chain mail with a sword at his side, a whole lot of sexy was on display, as well. Her heart did a crazy twist when Matt reached for the laces at her back.

Crap, don't picture him undoing the dress. Just... don't.

Dying to cover her nerves, she eyed him speculatively in the mirror. "Does this make you my lady-in-waiting?"

One side of his mouth curled up in amusement. "No," he said. "And before you get any other crazy ideas in your head, I'm nobody's knight in shining armor, either."

Matt's fingers whispered against her as he fixed the corset-inspired lace-up fastening in the back. Careful not to move, Callie concentrated on the warm brushes of skin on skin that sent currents of electric heat skittering up her spine. As touches went, this one bordered on being an incredible tease.

His gaze on the task at hand, lips set as if in concentration, Matt said, "You sure are going all out on this. I mean—" his eyes crashed into hers "—Tommy's *my* brother."

Callie blinked and mentally shoved her libido in a box. The most truthful explanation wouldn't go over so well, for sure.

Especially with Matt.

She held his gaze in the mirror. "They deserve the wedding of their dreams."

She'd never meant the words more, but she also knew reciting the slogan from her website didn't cover everything she'd poured into this event so far. And everything left yet to do. After talking with Tommy and Penny yesterday afternoon—they'd both sounded so sweet and sincere on the phone—Callie's heart had melted more.

In a way, her screwup had torn her and Colin apart. Years later, and she was *still* alone. Tommy's and Penny's screwups had led them to one another and now they were getting married. Their heartwarming story was one of the most inspiring Callie had ever heard. And she'd heard some doozies, stories of lost loves reunited and second chances and those who'd survived devastating illnesses to go and achieve their happily-ever-after.

But Tommy and Penny's tale of overcoming the effects of the bad choices they'd made struck a chord in Callie. After talking to the two, Callie's ideas for the weekend had exploded. So now there was more work than originally planned. Not that she feared hard work. In fact, she'd grown quite used to it.

But Matt clearly couldn't figure out why she'd brought more work on herself.

"I guess because I know what it's like to mess up your life," Callie said. "In college, I made some seriously stupid decisions."

The fingers on her back grew still, and Matt's eyes met hers in the mirror again. His gaze didn't budge as he remained silent, most likely waiting for her to go on. Callie's throat suddenly felt twice baked and lacking in all moisture.

"I let a lot of people down," she said. "Including my parents. And Colin."

"Tell me."

With those words, her immediate thought was *no* because the story was too personal, cut too close to the bone. But maybe if she shared the ugly truth about her past this would help Matt. She'd sensed there was tension between him and his brother. Maybe he'd find a way to move on, as well. The idea of her story helping others was kind of appealing.

Time to put your big-girl panties on, Callie.

Matt's focus dropped back to her dress and he resumed his task. Maybe he sensed that telling the story would be easier without his eyes studying her so closely. Despite his focus being elsewhere, she could tell by the tension in his shoulders and the set of his mouth that Matt's attention was solely on her.

She cleared her throat to loosen the muscles. "I grew up poor, in a little town north of here. My parents sacrificed a lot to move us to the city so I could go to a better high school. They wanted me to attend a university and be the first LaBeau to get a college degree."

"Did you have trouble in high school?"

"Nope. I did well," she said. "Straight-A student. I wound up with several acceptances to excellent schools. My parents wanted me to accept the scholarship at a smaller college closer to home, but I..."

Callie stared at her reflection in the mirror. She'd been so dumb, thinking her ability to adjust to a new high school translated into an easy adjustment to a new town and a large university.

"I wanted to get out and see the world," she said. "I mean, high school seemed fairly easy. How hard could an out-of-state larger university be? So I accepted the Wimbly Southern deal."

His gaze ticked back to hers in the mirror. "Scholarship?"

"A full ride," she said with a nod. "Tuition. Room and

board. Books. The works. Even some spending money so I didn't have to get a job. I only had to concentrate on my studies. For a girl with parents who could barely afford the rent, it was a big deal."

He cocked his head, the fingers at her back now motionless. "Let me guess. You flunked out and lost the scholarship."

Callie hesitated. She could say yes and let that be the end. His short sentence summed up the events accurately. But she knew leaving out the most important bits would be taking the coward's way out, and certainly wouldn't explain about her commitment to Matt's brother and his fiancée—a couple she'd only spoken to once on the phone.

"Yes, but there's a little more to the story," she said.

"How much more?"

"My grades slipped because I fell in with the wrong crowd. I was lonely, and the party kids were the only ones who would have anything to do with me."

In hindsight, she realized how lucky she'd been in high school. Moving just before the tenth grade should have meant she'd been the odd one out, friendless and alone. Instead, things had come together easily. She'd had plenty of friends and was well liked by her classmates. Some of that might have had to do with her dating Colin, his popularity rubbing off on her. Either way, things had fallen into place and she'd never missed a beat.

College, on the other hand, had been a disaster.

Callie cleared her throat. "But the party crowd comes with certain expectations, and I went out too much." She rolled her eyes. "That alone would have been enough for the Moron of the Year Award, but one night I went to a party at a house."

Matt's going to hate what comes next.

She gripped the skirt of her dress, wishing the silken folds could sooth her nerves, and she gathered her courage before she went on. "The police raided the place because the man was a drug dealer."

Matt sucked in a breath and his lips went white, and she knew the news had hit him viscerally. He looked as if he'd received a solid punch to the solar plexus. She whirled around to face him, laying a hand on his arm. Her heart pumped hard in her chest.

The rest tumbled out of her mouth. "I didn't know who he was or what he did to make money, Matt." She stared up at him, emphasizing every word and trying hard to convince him of the truth with her gaze. "He was a friend of a friend of a friend. It sounds like a stupid cliché, I know, but I honestly had no idea who the man was. But—"

She bit her cheek and held her tongue, staring at Matt. Callie shoved her hair back from her face, disturbed by the slight tremor in her fingers.

"We all got taken down to the station and…and they found marijuana in my purse."

"Jesus, Callie."

And then Matt just seemed to stop breathing, as if this final piece of the sordid story was just one insult too many. There was no way out but the truth. And the faster she got this over with, the sooner her heart would start beating again.

Callie drew in a shaky breath and pushed on. "I know. I *know*. I was stupid and depressed and I just wanted something to make it all go away. It was the only time, I swear."

The stupid move would follow her around the rest of her life. She briefly pressed her eyes closed. The shock of her arrest had been difficult enough for her, but it had been horrible for her parents. Years of being the perfect kid, the perfect student, had made her fall from grace all that much more painful. Especially given their car had been plastered with so many Student of the Week bumper stickers the chrome on the bumper had all but disappeared.

"I called my parents, who couldn't come to help me out, so they sent Colin." She winced at the memories of the complete and utter humiliation when Colin had strode into the police headquarters, clearly furious. "He drove up to Wimbly, even though I didn't ask him to," she said, realizing she was rambling again. "And then, of course, things between the two of us started to fall apart and I—"

The look on Matt's face gave no indication as to what he was thinking. The knot in her stomach tangled a little tighter, so she hurried on, beyond ready to push on to the next subject.

"I just think, after everything they've been through, Penny and Tommy deserve the wedding of the century," she said.

The tension in his body had eased a bit, and he leaned back against the wall, arms folded across the chain mail on his chest. For one bizarre moment, she realized she missed his hands on her skin. Callie smoothed her hand down the satiny skirt of the underdress.

"And if I can help Colin out with a fantastic publicity opportunity *and* prove to my parents my business is a success, all at the same time, so much the better."

Parked against the wall, Matt continued to study her.

She still couldn't tell what he was thinking. That she was an idiot? That she deserved to return to New Orleans, the stink of shame following on her heels? True.

But jeez, the whole mess had taken place ten years ago.

"Aren't you going to say anything?" she asked.

There was a two beat pause before he answered. "You're right." She held her breath as he went on. "The dress does flatten your breasts too much."

A bark of surprised laughter escaped Callie, one part humor and a hundred parts absolute relief. "Oh, my God, you really *are* a perv."

He smiled, crinkles appearing around his eyes, the tension of the moment finally broken. "Are we done with the confession now?"

Callie released her death grip on her skirt, muscles finally relaxing.

"Beyond done," she said.

"Good. Now could you please help me get this son of a bitch off?" He pulled at the chain-mail shirt a bit, letting it drop back to his chest with a *ching.* "I'm about to die of heat stroke here. And no way in hell do I want to pass out and be carted off to the nearest emergency room in this getup."

"Sure, turn around."

She spent a minute wrestling with the clasp at the nape of his neck, her fingers fumbling a bit as she tried to ignore the soft tickle of hair against her fingers. Against her will, awareness washed over her again, and her gaze slid past his broad shoulders down to his trim waist and lean hips. The body looked solid and rugged and was impossible to ignore, especially in the kind of getup that hinted at strong heroes, epic battles and undying devotion to a lady.

Ridiculous, Callie. You're absolutely ridiculous.

"Now face me and lean in," she said.

Matt turned and bent forward at the waist, and Callie pulled the hem up his trunk and over his head. The chain mail was heavier than it looked, pulling the shirt beneath along, as well. The whole ensemble dropped to the floor with a *clank* and Matt straightened up.

Holy hell. What had she done?

Now she had to hold herself together in the presence of a shirtless Matt with sexily mussed hair. While her heart thudded, Callie tried to drag her gaze from Matt's chest, but failed. The well-honed muscles had a dusting of hair that tapered at his waist, passing over the flat abdomen and disappearing beneath his pants.

A small smirk quirked his lips. "Are you checking out my cleavage?"

Several seconds passed before her brain could arrange the words in the right order. "You don't have man boobs."

"Good thing, too."

Time seemed to grind to a halt as they both studied each other. And then Matt stepped closer, with *goal* written all over his face, and the tension returned, ten times worse than before. But this time the air was filled with a sexual charge. Electric currents prickled just beneath her skin and spread, producing goose bumps as they went.

And her briefly returned ability to speak fled even faster than before.

"Only problem I see with this scenario?" He grabbed a fistful of fabric just beneath her fitted waist and slowly drew her closer, her pulse picking up speed with every step. "You are way overdressed."

Callie tried to protest. "The owner is—"

"Currently engrossed in a conversation with a customer about the history of Mardi Gras."

She blinked, trying to process all the input threatening to blow a fuse in her brain. Too many sparking impulses firing at once. Just the bare torso alone was enough to shove her senses into complete meltdown. But toss in the sight of all that lovely, lovely skin covering muscles and sinew and bone? The rudimentary pants clinging low on lean hips? She could just make out the top of his briefs. Blue.

Matt continued to slowly pull her forward, until her body finally met his—naked chest to, unfortunately, *not* naked chest. His eyes zeroed in on her lips, and several thoughts flashed through her brain at once.

This isn't why you're here, Callie. You need to stay focused on the job.

His mouth covered hers. And just like the focused man who'd hunted her down at the wedding reception, this man was all about the goal, as well. He tipped her head back and his lips pressed in firmly, opening Callie's mouth wide and taking his time with each retreat. Several deep, wet kisses followed. Forceful, yet unhurried. Heat and moisture and hard lips registered just before his tongue rasped against hers.

For a brief moment her mind splintered, and she moaned.

Matt gripped the fabric on the outside of her thighs, settling her legs on either side of his thighs. Unfortunately, the mounds of fabric between them prevented the satisfaction of feeling his hard body pressed against hers.

"Jesus," he muttered, arching his hip. "How the hell did people wear these bloody clothes?"

She gripped his arms, hoping to keep from melting into the floor. The fingers twisted tight in her dress hauled her that last little bit, and she had to adjust her stance to allow his leg to settle between her thighs. Then there was a skitter of pleasure up her spine from the pressure, the fabulously delicious *friction*…

My God.

She closed her eyes.

"Too bad my brother wasn't into *Space Vixens from the Planet Venus*," Matt said, nibbling his way from one side of her mouth to the other.

"Why would you say that?"

Geez, she sounded so breathless.

He dove in for another openmouthed kiss, and several mind-spinning seconds later he said, "Because their costumes were smaller. Much smaller."

Another drugging kiss consumed her, his tongue hot and demanding and doing unspeakable things to her body. His hand drifted to the small of her back to keep her pressed close. That leg pressed firmly against the part of her anatomy that desired the contact the most.

And those little rudimentary pants and thin briefs did nothing to hide the hard shaft pressed along her hip.

The sensation too fabulous to lose, she pulled herself a little higher up his leg, and the slow drag of fabric settled more firmly against the sensitive area between her thighs. Callie let out a whimper.

Good Lord. She needed to… She had to…

Matt's hands landed along her shoulder blades and began to undo those laces he'd worked so long and hard to fasten. As the back of the dress slowly fell open, cool air slid down her skin. The contact sent an illicit thrill skittering up her spine.

Surely she should be letting out some sort of protest? Where was her vow to keep her hands to herself? Where was her focus? Even more important, where was her sense of decency?

A loud laugh from somewhere in the store broke through Callie's lust-muddled brain, and they both went still. Callie silently counted to five and listened to Matt's harsh breaths before she gathered the strength to open her eyes.

Lips brushing against hers, he said, "I'm thinking we should fix our clothes."

Which totally was in contrast to the palm pressed flat against her back, holding her firmly against his chest.

"Um…yeah," she muttered against his lips, embarrassed by her less than brilliant response.

"What's on the agenda for tomorrow?" he said. "Searching out a pack of traveling circus performers to juggle flaming torches?"

Her lips smiled against his. Something about his teasing tone and his easygoing manner made the moment less awkward.

She stole a quick kiss before answering. "No," she said. "Though we do need to find someone who can transport a dragon from Colin's storage house to the park."

He pulled his head back and hiked a brow dryly. "Well, that shouldn't be hard at all."

"We're in New Orleans," Callie said. "This town

plans, produces and pulls off the Mardi Gras parade every year. There are plenty of people who can properly transport a dragon."

"So tomorrow will be about securing dragon transport?"

Callie opened her mouth to say yes and then bit her lip, remembering that her aunt had called this morning and asked for her help sorting through the stuff at the dock house. Callie had promised to drive up to Aunt Billie's place despite her suspicions the favor wasn't the real reason her aunt wanted Callie to visit.

While she was always pleased to see her favorite relative, the visit never came without a risk. But there was definitely a way to cut down on said risk. Bring backup. Provide a distraction, so to speak. Matt was the perfect person to help in that regard.

Callie eyed Matt. His hair was adorably tousled and his lips looked ruddy from their kisses. And something about his manner always put her at ease, even while revving up her body...

Talk about distractions.

"Actually," she said, "I have to head up to Clemence tomorrow. I was hoping you could ride along. I have to see my aunt Billie, and I think you should get out for an authentic taste of our cuisine and experience the bayou."

"Sightseeing wasn't really in my plans."

"But there's so much to see and this is your first trip to town. You can't come to New Orleans without sampling a little of rural Louisiana."

He tipped his head and looked down at her. Why was she holding her breath, hoping he'd say yes?

"Will there be mosquitos?" he asked.

"Big ones."

"Gators?"

"Most definitely."

"Dirt roads?"

"With potholes the size of Texas."

His lips twitched, as if fighting a smile. "Sounds enticing," he said dryly.

"On the bright side, my aunt makes the best shrimp étouffée in three counties. And she has a successful restaurant to show for it."

"Now that sounds good."

The response encouraging, Callie had to smile. "Hope you like it hot."

"Ms. LaBeau," Matt said, leaning close, his lips whispering across hers, "I like everything hot."

CHAPTER FOUR

THE TWO-HOUR drive up to Clemence, located north of Baton Rouge, passed pleasantly enough. At least, as pleasant as possible given Callie remained distracted, both by Matt's presence in her car and the destination.

As usual, the closer Callie drew to her old hometown the more her stomach filled with knots. Visiting Aunt Billie always managed to be fun and painful at the same time. Hopefully, with Matt along, Callie could avoid the painful part. From the first moment her family had learned of her mistake, her aunt had been her staunchest supporter, which always made Callie feel even worse for letting her down.

Once they'd finally left Baton Rouge behind, the roads grew narrower, quieter and lined with oaks. More important, now that they were getting close to Po Boy's, her aunt's restaurant, the roads were filled with the occasional pothole.

"Man," Matt said as he steered around one. "You weren't kidding about the condition of the roads." He glanced into his rearview mirror. "That one should be named Grand Canyon, the junior."

The conversation was as good a lead-in as she'd ever get. "So what's it like where you're from?" Callie asked.

She twisted in the passenger seat of her car and leaned back against the door to better study Matt as he steered her car down the road. "Where do you live again?"

"Manford, Michigan."

Which hardly answered the question burning in her brain. She hiked a brow, encouraging him to go on.

Two beats passed before he answered. "Midsize town. We have a mall, a couple of movie theatres and the hospital is decent enough. Though the emergency room isn't as big as I'd like."

Something in his tone told her that last statement represented a massive understatement.

"I thought you worked as a traveling doc," she said.

He cleared his throat. "I have a part-time job at Manford Memorial. That allows me enough free time to travel as a locums, picking up shifts in bigger cities."

"If you prefer living in a larger city, why are you living there?"

Several seconds ticked by. "It's home." He gave a shrug, the act as vague as his words.

But his voice gave him away, the lack of excitement almost palpable. Callie loved New Orleans, loved everything about the town that managed to merge quirky and a unique cultural heritage with its own brand of Southern charm, all at the same time. The city merged the concepts with a kind of easy grace that amazed her, every single time, and provided the perfect backdrop for her business. Despite the strained relationships, her family was here, too. She'd grown up in the area and couldn't imagine living anywhere else.

Matt, apparently, had little affection for his own town.

"Promise me something," she said, and he looked

at her curiously. "No matter what happens, don't go to work for the Manford Chamber of Commerce doing tourist promotion, because you would really suck at the job."

Matt laughed, and she admired the strong throat, the even, white teeth. His sandy, tousled hair that begged to be ruffled, and Callie flexed her fingers against the urge to reach over and run her fingers through his hair.

In an attempt to dodge a pothole on the left, Matt steered the Toyota to the right, and the front tire hit a second pothole. He shot her a look, and Callie lifted a shoulder. "You get used to it."

He glanced at her from the corner of his eye. "You grew up out here?"

"Yep," she said. "Born right here in Clemence Parish. Spent my childhood playing in the water, fishing and catching crawfish."

"A tomboy?"

"And proud of it."

She pointed out the turns, the roads growing narrower, until finally they hit the dirt road that dead-ended into Po Boy's. There were a half dozen or so cars in the gravel parking lot, shaded by huge oaks, and Matt pulled into a spot in the front.

They exited and rounded the car. Matt came to a stop to stare up at the wooden building.

"Aunt Billie's restaurant looks…interesting."

Callie grinned at the expression on his face. The paint on the siding was peeling and cracked, the wood beneath faded to gray where exposed to the sun. The front porch held several tables and chairs, but Callie knew the customers preferred the back and the view of the river.

"Authentic," she said.

He hiked a brow. "Safe?"

She bit back a smile. "Absolutely."

They made their way up the wooden front steps. Matt's hand settled into the dip in her spine, and the heat seeped through her shirt and warmed her skin. Unfortunately, the temperature change didn't stop there. The feeling settled deeper, curling low in her stomach and spreading between her legs. Good Lord. Yesterday's dressing-room incident had clearly left an indelible impression.

They stepped into the restaurant filled with wooden tables and chairs and a few customers. As usual, Aunt Billie sensed her arrival before Callie had taken ten steps inside.

Her aunt appeared from the doorway leading into the kitchen. "Callie, hon. It's been way too long." She enveloped her in a hug before gripping Callie's arms and pulling back to give her the once-over.

Billie LaBeau loved to cook, loved to eat and she had the well-padded frame of one who did. But her generous nature dwarfed everything else in comparison. Despite the distance in the lineage, Aunt Billie took her Creole roots to heart. More important, she'd been the only relative to accept Callie's choices, without treating her life as if she'd settled for a seriously lower second best.

Not once had she looked at Callie with disappointment or thrown out little asides that alluded to how much Callie had screwed up. And while she constantly harped at Callie to visit more often, there was never any judgment in her tone.

"This is Matt Paulson," Callie said.

"'Bout time you brought a man around here again."

Billie shot her a grin. "Haven't done so since Colin. And you were eighteen years old then."

The implied *ten years ago* went unsaid and Callie fought the urge to close her eyes. Perhaps Matt's presence wouldn't be quite the protection that she'd hoped.

"Matt is a *client*," Callie said.

Hopefully the emphasis on the word would clear up any misconceptions. Aunt Billie's only response was a raised eyebrow at Matt's hand on Callie's back, sending heat shooting up Callie's neck and flaring across her cheeks. Who needed to say anything with a facial expression like her aunt's? Matt was studying Callie, clearly amused by the conversation and the nonverbal communication.

"Welcome, Matt," Aunt Billie said. "I hope you brought your appetite."

"I never leave home without it."

Aunt Billie let out an amused snort. "That's good to hear. And Callie?" Aunt Billie returned her focus to Callie. "The family reunion is in two weeks. It's not too late to change your mind and attend."

Crap, the reunion. She'd forgotten about the annual event that she had no intention of attending, *ever*. She couldn't imagine anything worse than all the family members—those who'd been so proud she'd been accepted to Wimbly—talking about her behind her back. Mentioning her mistake again to her face. Callie had lost count of how many times she'd been told how lucky she was to be afforded the opportunity.

Many of whom now never missed an opportunity to remind her of how much she'd lost when she'd mucked it all up.

Her aunt propped a hand on her ample hip. "I'd love to have all of my family back in the same place again."

"Maybe," Callie said vaguely. "My schedule is pretty busy. I'll have to check the dates."

The look her aunt sent made her message clear. She didn't believe Callie would show up, and Billie sure as heck wouldn't pass up the opportunity to hound her more. Her suspicions about her aunt's recent call to sort through her stuff from the dock house suddenly didn't seem so paranoid. Billie hadn't suddenly been bitten by a late-summer spring-cleaning urge to clean out an old building that seldom got used anymore. She'd planned on slowly eroding away Callie's excuses.

But the thought of all her relatives looking at her as if she'd failed…

Damn it.

"Well, check them dates and try a little harder to squeeze your family into that busy schedule of yours, ya' hear?" Billie said.

"Work has been busy."

"All the more reason you need to come back for a visit," Billie said. "Let your people know how you're doing."

Callie murmured something polite and vague. Billie shot her a sharp look and then seemed to give up, letting the subject go. They spent some time catching up as Billie gave Matt a tour of the kitchen, showing him around and dolling out her blunt brand of humor as they went. Callie liked the laid-back way Matt dodged her aunt's repeated attempts to nail down the details about their relationship. Finally, her aunt seemed to realize that there would be nothing more forthcoming.

"I finally decided to send someone out to do the repairs on the dock house. The stuff inside needs to be sorted, too," Aunt Billie said. "And since you're the only one that goes out there anymore, I need to know what you want me to keep and what I can toss."

A wave of affection hit Callie, and she reached out to gently squeeze her aunt's hand. "Thanks."

She knew her aunt would have torn the thing down by now if not for her. And losing the dock house would be like losing a piece of herself.

"But first, y'all take a seat out on the deck and I'll bring you some lunch," Billie said.

Callie couldn't resist and she sent her aunt a smile. "Make sure you make Matt's shrimp étouffée extra special."

They settled at a table out back, the edge of the deck lined by the Mississippi River. Despite the rustic surroundings, Matt appeared totally at ease. She liked that he seemed comfortable no matter where he was, whether at a classy ice bar or a backwoods restaurant. They settled into easy conversation, which ended when Aunt Billie brought sweet tea and two bowls of shrimp étouffée. Callie watched with satisfaction as Matt took his first bite, eyelids stretching wide. To his credit he swallowed and appeared completely unflustered as he reached for his iced tea before taking a sip.

For some reason, she couldn't resist. Matt Paulson brought out the flirt in her.

"I thought you liked it hot," she said.

The deep, throaty chuckle sent a shocking shiver up her spine. When was the last time a man's laugh made her this...*aware?* Because that was the only word to describe the feeling vibrating just beneath the surface of her skin. Like a potential lightning bolt loomed close and the hairs on her arms lifted in anticipation, expecting the strike at any moment.

To cover, she pulled out her notebook. She still liked to handwrite her initial to-do list before entering information into her laptop later. There was something about the physical act of writing that always got her creative side going. While they ate, Callie went over where things stood for the LARP weekend.

Matt never said a word outside of answering her questions, finishing his bowl of étouffée without a complaint. By the end, sweat dotted his temple, and he reached for his iced tea regularly, but, after that first look of shock…nothing.

When he shoved his bowl back, he sent her a smile.

"Did I pass the LaBeau initiation right?"

Callie propped her elbows on the table. "You did," she said. "With flying colors, too."

A waitress refilled their iced-tea glasses and cleared their lunch dishes away. Matt took a sip of his tea, eyeing her over his glass, and an uncomfortable feeling prickled the back of her neck.

He set his glass down. "How come you refuse to come back to your family reunion?"

"I didn't refuse. I…" She pressed her lips together and slid her gaze out over the river. "I just don't have time."

"Bull," he said softly.

She ticked her gaze back to his. "It is always easy to question the judgment of others in matters of which we may be imperfectly informed.'"

Matt lifted a brow. "Mr. Darcy again?"

"No. His love interest, Elizabeth Bennet. You should read the book."

"Maybe someday," he said with a chuckle. But clearly he wasn't about to be derailed from the topic at hand. "Some people aren't lucky enough to have any family, Callie," he said, and guilt stabbed her in the gut. "Seems a waste for you to avoid yours."

She opened her mouth to defend herself, feeling uncomfortable. She couldn't formulate an intelligent response so she tried another diversionary tactic instead.

"You ready to go for a ride in my boat?" she said.

The raise of his eyebrow let her know he was on to her, but then his grin turned positively sinful. "Is that what they're calling it these days?"

The suggestion slid through her and stirred her blood, but she remained outwardly calm as she played dumb. "I don't know what you're talking about."

"I was hoping there was a hidden meaning in that question," he asked.

He leaned forward and crossed his arms on the tiny table, his face mere inches from her face. A jolt of awareness shot through her body. The proximity sent a skitter of nerves just beneath her skin.

Hazel. His eyes were hazel.

For a moment, intrigued by the discovery, she couldn't respond.

She'd thought his eyes were brown. Of course their first meeting had taken place outside at dusk, with the only lights offered those of fake kerosene lamps. At the park she hadn't gotten close enough to tell, and during the brain-meltingly hot moment in the dim fitting room she'd been distracted by that hard chest on display. But now, in the full light of day, and with them so close, she could make out the yellow and green specks mixed in with the brown.

"Nope. No hidden messages," she said. "I thought I'd show you where I used to go fishing as a kid. But I *really* want to see how the guy who prefers the city deals with a boat ride in backcountry Louisiana."

"Is this another initiation rite?"

A grin slid up her face. "Maybe," she said. "Think you can handle it?"

"I can handle anything you've got."

Fighting words if she'd ever heard them.

Her brow hiked higher. "Cocky, aren't you?"

He tipped back his head and laughed. And once again she was presented with a vision of a strong throat and even, white teeth. The laugh lines around his eyes weren't as deep as his thirty years would suggest. And Callie wondered if that meant his smile rarely made it all the way to his eyes.

"Because I'm that kind of guy, I'll let the obvious comeback for that question slide buy."

"A sign of intelligence."

"Well—" he stood up "—let's get the rest of this family hazing over with."

When they went back inside the restaurant, Aunt Billie wouldn't let him pay, of course. Callie smothered the smile as Matt wasted ten minutes trying to change her mind, without success. Callie's grin finally appeared as she watched Matt wait for Aunt Billie to return to the kitchen before he passed by their table and left enough to cover the bill plus a very generous tip. The man never came up against a problem he couldn't solve.

And what would she do if he finally turned that determination on her?

* * *

Fighting the doubt, Matt hooked his hands on his hips and stared down at the old fiberglass boat tied to the wooden dock. "You sure this thing is safe?"

"Of course it is."

Callie, loose-limbed and agile, ignored the tiny ladder fixed to the side of the deck and hopped inside the boat with the grace of a cat. Beneath her cut-offs, toned, tanned legs ended in delicate sandals. Her beautiful shoulders now on display beneath a feminine T-shirt. Opposed to Friday night's arrangement, her hair hung loose.

And, as promised, a heat wave had settled on top of the delta. The muggy temperature was stifling. Although her T-shirt was damp, her face slightly flushed, she didn't appear bothered.

Man, how did the woman handle the weather and still look so cool?

She turned and looked up at him, a smile on her lips and a challenge in her eyes. "Don't you trust me?"

His lips twitched. "Only to a certain extent."

Eyes twinkling, Callie remained silent and sent him an I-dare-you hike of her brow. After a moment's hesitation, Matt let out a light scoff and climbed down into the boat.

"Feel free to drive," she said. "I get the feeling you like to be the one steering the boat."

"Was that a metaphor?" Matt said as he sat in the driver's seat.

"Definitely."

Surprisingly, the outboard motor of the flat-bottomed boat started easily, and Matt realized that, despite being old, the boat had been carefully maintained. Given the earlier conversation with her aunt, he got the distinct feeling Callie used it more than anyone else.

Curious about why, he steered up the canal while studying the woman up front. Callie had stretched out on the bench on the bow, eyes closed and face tilted into the breeze, obviously enjoying the wind in her hair. In the bright light he could make out streaks of gold mixed with the honey-colored strands.

The towering cypress trees lining the canal blocked most of the direct light, but the lazy heat sat on them relentlessly, the air smelling of damp earth. Spanish moss hung like tinsel in a Christmas tree, adding more of an eerie mood than a festive one.

Matt settled back in his seat, surprised at the stillness of their surroundings. Other than the ripples from their boat, and the quiet purr of the small motor, nothing moved or made a sound. Several minutes passed with the boat following the serpentine path. They rounded a curve and a lake opened out before them. Ten minutes later Callie pointed Matt in the direction of a small boathouse on stilts, blending with the trees.

"Here we are."

Matt hopped up onto the porch that also served as a high dock. Beside the wooden structure a large rope hammock—looking brand-new and out of place next to the ancient building—stretched invitingly between two oak trees. After securing the boat, he reached down and pulled Callie up onto the dock.

"I hadn't planned on taking the time to sightsee while in New Orleans." And yet, here he stood in the middle of friggin' nowhere, all because he hadn't had the will-power to resist a day with Callie. "But if I had made plans, I certainly would have chosen something a little less…" He stared across the cypress-tree-lined lake and the lapping water. The endless stretch of nothing but water and trees. "Wild."

"I promise," she said, grinning up at him, "when we get back I'll take you out on the town and show you the best New Orleans has to offer, like a nice dinner out. A little dancing. And if you're really lucky, maybe even a tour of my condo. But until then—" She backed up slowly toward the edge of the dock, flipping off her sandals and slipping her watch from her wrist, leaving Matt uneasy. The light in her eyes set him on edge in ways that weren't safe to consider.

"Where are you going?" Matt asked. A thrum of anxiety curled in Matt's stomach, and he looked out at the water. "I don't think—"

"Holler when you see a gator." And with that, Callie pivoted and dove into the water.

The splash came, raining cool drops on Matt's face and shirt, and he nearly groaned at the brief relief from the heat. In her T-shirt and shorts, Callie swam toward the center of a clearing beneath the low-hanging branches of several cypress trees and turned to tread water, smiling up at him.

"You coming in?" she said. "It's the final LaBeau initiation rite."

"What the hell do I get in return for passing all these tests?"

A smile crept up her face. "A permanent spot at the family table at Po Boy's."

"If you're not going to be there, then what's the point?"

She shot him a you're-not-funny look, and he decided to let the issue slide.

"Besides," he said, "I'm not sure that's an honor the lining of my esophagus would survive."

"I told Aunt Billie to make yours extra hot."

He tipped his head as the realization hit him. "Yours wasn't as hot as mine?"

"Nope. Can't stand it spicy. I always order it mild." The playful light in her eyes was almost worth suffering through étouffée that could be used to strip paint from wood.

Almost.

"Coming in?" she asked.

He stared down at her, hands on his hips, and a smile tugged at his lips. "Promise this is the last of the La-Beau family torture?"

"Last one, I swear."

"Okay," he said.

The woman clearly felt in her element. And while he might be a bit of a fish out of water in the backwoods of Louisiana, there were still some things that he controlled. Showing the lovely Ms. LaBeau a thing or two suddenly seemed incredibly important.

And too much fun to pass up.

After the years of worry and fear and sacrifice, he suddenly felt the urge to indulge in something just for himself. A moment to be something more than just a doctor, a brother and a stand-in parent. It had been far too long since he'd had sex, and today he was going to leave his many roles behind, save one: that of a red-blooded man in the company of a beautiful woman.

He flipped open his snap. To her credit, she didn't react except for a slight flaring of her eyelids as she continued to tread water. As Callie stared up at him, he struggled to keep the amusement from his face as he slid the zipper down. He waited for her to say something. A protest. A sound of encouragement. A mocking comment. Or, at the very least, a flicker of her gaze away from him.

Nothing.

Instead, Callie kept treading water, eyes on Matt as he hooked his hands in his shorts and shoved them down, kicking them aside. His briefs clung to his hips and, for a nanosecond, he considered shucking them, too. But he wasn't prepared for the likely ending to a bout of skinny-dipping. For one split second he mentally kicked himself for not considering the need for condoms. But right now the sun beat down on his back and sweat trickled between his shoulder blades and the water looked cool. Even better, the expression on Callie's face was inviting.

He executed a shallow dive, slicing through the water, and broke the surface just two feet from where Callie continued to tread water.

Her cheeks were flushed, whether from the heat or the sight of him in nothing but briefs, he wasn't sure.

"You know," she said dryly, "I wasn't kidding before. There are gators in these waters. So you best keep all your dangly bits inside your underwear."

He laughed, secretly pleased with the first words out of her mouth. "Thanks for the warning."

Matt fought the urge to cup her neck and drag her close for another kiss. Memories of their time in the fitting room that first night flooded his mind. The taste of her mouth, the feel of her hip.

Good thing the water was fairly cool because spontaneous combustion felt like a possibility. Unfortunately, despite being a strong swimmer he couldn't figure out how to follow through on the impulse to take that mouth in the way he wanted without drowning them both. Instead, he stretched out on his back to float, biding his time until she climbed out of the water and onto the dock. In wet clothes.

Just thinking about the sight made his groin grow tight.

Pushing the thought from his mind, he stared up at the canopy of cypress trees and the sunlight peeking through the leaves, letting the peaceful scene wash over him. For the ten years since his parents had died and he'd assumed responsibility of Tommy, he'd been living life on edge. The roller-coaster ride of Tommy's addiction had worn him out, leaving him constantly braced for the next bad happening. Taking a moment to just relax was a revelation.

"This is nice," he said.

He turned his head and met Callie's face just a few feet from his, also floating.

"I love Louisiana." Her smile wrinkled her nose in a way that could only be described as cute. "Never want to live anywhere else."

What would that be like? To live where you wanted, instead of where you had to?

He'd been stuck with Manford as his home base for so long, looking after Tommy, that he couldn't imagine a life anywhere else. But nothing about his hometown appealed to him. Never had. Never would. He'd grown up there dying to get out. But when his parents had died during his third year of college, he'd had no choice but to transfer back home before his senior year. To attend medical school and complete his E.R. residency in Detroit. Commuting as much as he could.

Sleeping in the on-call room when too tired to make the drive back home.

Sometimes he wondered if his brother's life would have turned out differently had Matt been around more during Tommy's early years of college.

He hated those self-defeating thoughts.

"But as much as I love New Orleans—" Callie's hand brushed his "—every once in a while I have to get out of town and come back here. It's so…peaceful."

They continued to float for a few more minutes, and every muscle in Matt's body slowly relaxed, until he truly felt like a floater, washed up on the beach. No tension. No worries about what tomorrow would bring.

A distant rumble of thunder broke the peace and sent them swimming for shore. Matt reached the dock first, hauling himself up. He turned and leaned down to take Callie's hand, pulling her up onto the dock… and straight into his arms.

He made no pretense that his actions were an accident. He dragged her dripping body up against his, until the wet T-shirt pressed so enticingly against her breasts was plastered against his chest. His body let out a sigh of relief.

"I've been thinking about this since the dressing room," he said.

She leaned back and eyed him. "I'm guessing your thoughts didn't include a dock house and a battered deck."

"The setting is irrelevant."

Since their kisses in the costume-shop dressing room, Matt hadn't been able to think of much else besides getting Callie back in his arms. And now that he had her here, he was going to take full advantage.

He swooped in for a kiss, gathering those soft lips against his, and a tiny moan escaped Callie. The sound shot straight to his groin.

Matt pressed his hand to the back of her head and molded himself more firmly against her. Water dripped from Callie's hair, landing on his arms, and Matt was surprised the drops didn't hit his overheated skin and fizzle into vapor. The taste and the feel of Callie in his arms were just as good as he remembered. He touched his tongue to her lower lip, and she opened her mouth wide, letting him inside. But, good God, this time it wasn't enough.

Ignoring the warning voices in his head, he lifted Callie into his arms. When she wrapped her legs around his waist, her body just brushed the top of his hard shaft. This time the groan came from him.

"Callie—"

He eyed the scene and then, decision made, headed for the hammock. Callie pressed herself more firmly against Matt.

"Callie."

She wasn't helping his self-control here.

He tumbled her back onto the hammock, the action creating a gentle rocking motion, and caught his weight with his hand. He stared down into brown eyes framed with thick lushes, wet from their swim.

"I'm not prepared for this." Even as he said the words, he stretched out beside her, covering that soft body with his own. The smell of shampoo—magnolia scented, maybe?—came from her hair.

Stupid, really, to torture himself this way. He pressed his forehead to hers. "I just want to enjoy holding you for a moment." His lips tipped up at the edges. "Minus the audience on the other side of a dressing-room door."

"I figured the perv finally wanted to cop a feel."

The image of doing exactly that left Matt's chuckle sounding strained. When Callie shifted slightly beneath him, pressing more of that soft body against his, the amusement died on his lips.

"Whatever we do," he said, "we leave the clothes *on.* I don't have a condom, but I know I'd have a devil of a time focusing on the technicalities if you were naked."

Matt swiped his hand down her side, cupping her thigh, and she closed her eyes. "So the clothes stay on," she said. "Got it."

The verbal agreement spiked his pulse higher, and he pressed her mouth open again with his, finally realizing the honey-colored hair and the honey drawl matched her honey taste.

Jesus, he needed to touch her.

He unsnapped her cutoffs and flattened his palm low against her slender belly.

"Matt." She arched her back in invitation, pressing closer, her eyes still closed. "I thought we'd agreed about the clothes—"

"We did. I'm not taking them off," he said. "I just want to touch you."

He fumbled briefly at the edge of her panties, cursing softly along the way. Why the hell was he so clumsy? But the need rushing through his veins made his fingers feel too hot and too eager and too greedy to go slow.

Matt shifted and tilted his head to take more of Callie's mouth as he finally succeeded in slipping his hand beneath the elastic band, seeking out the sweet spot that would bring about the response he craved. If he couldn't take exactly what he was dying for, then he wanted to hear Callie calling his name. He knew the flush staining her cheeks now had nothing to do with the heat wave. Goose bumps peppered her skin as he slid his palm lower with a purpose.

When he reached his goal, the soft folds beneath his fingers, Callie arched against him.

"Matt." She reached for his arms, her eyes wide. "I need—"

"I know what you need."

Callie gripped his forearm and he paused, refusing to give up his position, before stroking her between her legs.

With a groan, Callie closed her eyes. "That's mighty presumptuous of you."

"At this point," he said dryly. "I don't think either of us is thinking much beyond the big O."

She sounded out of breath. "You're too goal-oriented."

"Isn't that the point of all this?"

"The point is," she said, shifting a little lower down his chest, "to enjoy the journey en route."

And then Callie's hand landed on his hard-on, and Matt sucked in a breath and froze. The images ricocheting around his head included one of him shucking her pants and sliding between her thighs. But the one that wreaked the most havoc was of Callie's face, eyes dreamy and jaw slack as he thrust hard and brought them both to a rousing finale.

"Callie. I'm not sure—"

She tunneled her hand beneath his underwear.

"You're not sure of what?" she said, and she began

to stroke him through the cotton briefs, sending a stab of pleasure down his groin and searing his skin.

The urge to roll over and pin Callie beneath him sent a small shudder down his spine.

Matt let out an undignified curse. "I'm not sure this is wise."

She smiled against his mouth and then gave his lower lip a little nip. "If you get to touch me, then I get to touch you."

Well, hell, who could argue with logic like that?

Matt had just about adjusted to the fingers stroking him through the cotton when she ran her finger across the sensitive head, pulling an embarrassing groan from his mouth.

"Hmm," she murmured. "That was fun. Let's see if I get the same response again."

Matt left her lips and ran his mouth down the curve of her breast toward the center. The wet layer of cotton and the lace beneath were frustrating, but he continued to nip, placing sucking kisses along the path from one side to the other. He flicked his tongue across the tip, the partial bud growing fuller in response, and he grinned. Her fingers on his erection fumbled a little, and her free hand gripped the short hair at the back of his neck, pulling his head up until they were face-to-face.

The wide pupils and parted mouth were a beautiful sight, right before she dove in for a soul-searing kiss that almost had him losing his focus, his fingers briefly losing their rhythm beneath her pants.

"Here's an idea," he said, his voice throatier than he would have liked. "Let's see who can stay the most focused."

Eyelids wide, she said, "Clothes stay on?"

"Deal."

Matt knew he was in trouble when Callie stopped kissing him and pulled back to look at his face. Her lips—ruddy from being consumed by his—curled into a grin and, before Matt could figure out what she had in mind, her hand slipped beneath his briefs and made contact, closing around his erection. Her soft palm encircled his hard length.

For a moment, his mind went blank and his heart flatlined.

"Callie." This time her name came out more of a groan. "I can't—"

Callie writhed against him, encouraging his fingers to get with the program again. Desperate, he used his free hand to ruck her shirt up to just beneath her breasts before he caught himself, remembering their deal.

Why'd he come up with this torture?

Matt bent forward and captured the tip of her breast with his mouth again, cursing the two layers of fabric between them. Callie's hand stroked him faster, and the need building low in his back began to increase in intensity, his movements less about teasing and more about pushing them both over the edge. And the devouring of her with his lips and teeth and tongue became as much about satisfying his need as hers.

Callie's lids went wide, her mouth partially open as she sucked in breath after breath, and her hand began to falter, the rhythm of her strokes stuttering. When she arched her back, her body giving one final shudder, she dragged her thumb directly over his sensitive tip. Matt's spine went stiff, the orgasm shooting through him, stripping the strength from his limbs.

Matt had no idea how many minutes passed before

his endorphin-soaked brain became aware of his surroundings again. A breeze gently rocked the hammock and cooled their sweat-slicked skin. The smell of sex hung in the air, and the feel of Callie's soft body pressed against Matt's lulled him into a sense of peace. In fact, he might have sworn never to move again.

"That was definitely the most fun I've ever had with my clothes on," he said, his eyes still closed. "I haven't done the third-base-only thing since high school."

"Third base. Really? Do people still use the term?"

He looked down at Callie with a grin. "Only perverts like me."

She tipped back her head and laughed, and the movement sent their slick torsos sliding against each other.

"Um…" Callie wiggled against the mess between them as a small smile crept up her face. "I think we're going to need to go for another dip in the water."

CHAPTER FIVE

THE NEXT MORNING, Callie leaned back in the chair in her office and stared blankly at her laptop, currently parked on her desk. She'd come to work early to get some planning done, but after the hot moment in the hammock yesterday, her mind hadn't been the same. Her *body* hadn't been the same. How could she concentrate on creating a medieval menu for a wedding reception when all she could think about was Matt?

Especially getting Matt…*naked.*

They'd driven back to the city, and the parting had been full of untapped potential. Unfortunately she'd had a meeting with a client last evening, so she couldn't invite him up to her condo. And no matter how far things had gone between the two of them, she still felt awkward asking him to come to her place once she was free. A request synonymous with asking him over for a night of sex.

Not that there was anything wrong with *that.*

After all, they were two consenting adults.

However, if her current mind frame were any indication, having Matt Paulson around would surely slow down her progress at work.

Callie set her elbow on her sleek cherrywood desk

and propped her chin in her hand. Perhaps Matt was right. Maybe she should stop avoiding the extended family. Maybe if she simply started showing up to the various family functions her relatives would stop continuing to file her away under the to-be-pitied category. Avoiding the family while waiting for time to take care of the issue hadn't helped.

For God's sake, ten years surely would have cured the problem by now.

But continuing to avoid the family amounted to everyone thinking she was hiding in shame, which couldn't be further from the truth. She needed to show up, hold her head high and let everyone see that she was exactly where she wanted to be in her life, past mistakes be damned.

Callie sat up and fired off an email to her aunt, accepting the invitation to the family reunion. If she was lucky, maybe Matt would still be around and she could ask him to come with her. A little steadying presence by her side would be welcome for sure. Of course, having him around meant they could actually make it beyond the juvenile label of third base.

Unfortunately, the thought of Matt in her bed sidetracked her again.

"Callie."

Startled, she looked up. Colin stood on the other side of her desk, looking down at her with a bemused expression on his face, dark hair curling a bit just above his ears. How had he entered her office without her even hearing him? After a quick check of her watch, she realized fifteen minutes had passed by without her knowledge. Good Lord, she'd never get anything done at this rate.

"I knocked, but you didn't answer," Colin said.

"Sorry." Callie sat up and pretended to shuffle through a few files on her desk. "What have I done to warrant a visit from my favorite ex-boyfriend?"

Colin let out a huff of humor and dropped into the seat across from her. "I'd take that as a compliment if you had more exes running around."

Callie lifted a brow dryly, determined to remain unaffected by the efficiently targeted, well-meaning jab. Unfortunately, when Colin went on, remaining unaffected became impossible.

Colin crossed his arms. "The Paulson thing is turning into a bigger deal than I thought."

Oh, God.

Stunned, Callie stared at her ex, hoping to read exactly what he was talking about in his expression. But nothing in his blue eyes gave away his thoughts. Had he already guessed she was slipping quickly into a *thing,* for lack of a better word, with Matt? Callie racked her brain trying to figure out how she'd given everything away. Short of Matt leaving handprints on her body she was at a loss to explain the turn of events. Unless Colin had suddenly developed psychic powers she didn't know about.

"Uh...bigger deal?" she said.

"Yes. Like nationally televised newsworthy deal."

Television?

Matt *would* look good on a sex tape.

"Wait, *what?*" She shook her head and leaned back in her seat, trying to pry her mind out of the gutter. "I'm confused."

Clearly Colin was talking about something other than her relationship with Matt. Their sexual exploits, while hot in a kind of innocent way, were hardly the stuff of tabloids.

"The *Dungeons of Zhorg* community caught wind of the Paulson wedding," Colin said. "And there are people clamoring to come for some of the events."

Callie stared at her ex, her heart working overtime to supply enough blood to her brain. She'd only been gone for a day. One day. She'd enjoyed lunch with Matt, taken a swim and indulged in an erotic, fully clothed moment with a handsome guy. When the heck had everything become so crazy?

Being caught up in a sex-tape scandal suddenly seemed appealing in comparison.

"The LARP event was to be for the wedding guests only," Callie said.

"That was the original idea. But someone at Gamer's World got wind of the plans and now they want in on the action, too. I called and spoke with Tommy Paulson myself, and he and his fiancée are in favor of making this as big as we want, as long as Rainstorm Games foots the bill for all the extras. Our publicist is contacting the local networks and several of them are interested in running a human interest piece about Tommy and Penny's story."

Gamer's World? Networks?

Holy hell.

"Colin." Her voice came out weak. News cameras? At a wedding she'd arranged? "I only agreed to handle this wedding because the smaller scale made it doable. Money isn't the only issue here. I'm just one person, plus a part-time assistant."

And while the businesswoman in her considered the additions an opportunity of a lifetime, the woman who wanted to have time to eat and sleep over the next two months had issues with the idea. Not to mention how would she even find two minutes to see where yesterday's foray into hotness with Matt would lead? And see where the relationship would take her?

"Don't worry," he said. "I have plenty of experience with these types of events. I've launched several popular games, remember?"

"What I remember best was you arranging a zombie invasion of a wedding your wife and I planned," she said dryly.

Colin sent her an unapologetic grin.

Despite everything, she smiled. "It was an epic ending to a fabulous wedding."

Callie had gone all out in helping Colin's then-fiancée plan a spectacular Mardi Gras wedding. She'd grown pretty close to Jamie in the process. And even though Callie wished them well in their marital bliss, a little part of Callie envied them, as well. The closest Callie had ever come to anything serious had been with Colin, and their relationship ended ten years ago.

I'd take that as a compliment if you had more exes running around.

The realization suddenly made her love life seem a little pathetic. But she'd been so busy pouring all her energies into her business, determined to turn her negative into a positive that she hadn't had time for a relationship.

She hadn't lived the life of a monk. She wasn't *that* insane. Callie had dated and enjoyed herself along the way. But she'd passed on actively pursuing anything serious because she wanted to be in the right place in her life. And while she'd been building her business, her social life had lagged behind, stuck in the old days.

Hanging out with old friends was well and good, but what about making new ones?

Case in point, one of her best friend's was her ex from ten years ago.

Unfortunately, Colin seemed oblivious to her brutal personal epiphany as he went on.

"I checked out the park you chose and spoke with the people in charge," he said. "They have plenty of room and more than adequate parking."

Right. They were in the middle of discussing how her work life had just gotten hellaciously complicated. Did he have any idea what he was asking of her?

Colin went on. "I don't think we'll need that much room, but the park said they could handle up to a thousand people."

"A thousand?" she said weakly, trying to force her mind back to the concerning turn of events. Her private party wedding suddenly going public…

"Colin, that's way more work than I signed on for."

"I know you've been trying to prove to your parents how successful your business has become. I assumed you'd jump at the chance to do exactly that."

"True. But televising a wedding I've only had two months to arrange isn't exactly how I figured to pull this off."

"If anyone can do this, it's you."

"You mean if anyone is crazy enough to *try,* it's me."

"Listen, Callie—" Colin leaned forward, his blue eyes on hers "—I trust you. I know you can pull this off in a manner that will live up to the newly expanded LARP event."

I trust you.

Damn, here she was resenting the fact he'd just increased her workload by a hundred and he had the nerve to utter those words she rarely heard other than from her clients.

I trust you.

The twinge in her heart was impossible to ignore.

After her spectacular fail in college, the one person she'd directly affected the most had been Colin. She hadn't asked him to come up and bail her out. But he'd come. Because that was the kind of guy he was. And the trip had cost him greatly.

Still, he'd been the first to forgive her. The first to embrace her crazy decision to start her own business arranging themed weddings, and he even managed her website. And if that wasn't enough, he participated in the *Ex Factor* blog because it helped *her,* not him. He remained anonymous, which meant he received nothing in return, other than the satisfaction of seeing his friend succeed and her massive gratitude.

Callie stared at Colin. Obviously Colin considered the turn of events an opportunity not to be missed, for both her business and his. And Tommy and Penny appeared thrilled, as well.

"When it comes to work, no one is more focused than you, Callie."

I was until Matt Paulson landed in my life.

"Uh, thanks."

Clearly the man didn't remember how distracted she'd been when he'd arrived at her office. And all of this meant that, damn, she probably should try to tone things down with the brother of the groom. How could she give this event the proper attention while preoccupied by the potential for more with Matt Paulson?

"You know I'll give it my all," she said.

"You always do." Colin reached across her desk and gave her a friendly cuff on the arm. "I'll have my publicist coordinate things with you. And if you need any extra help, don't hesitate to holler."

She sent him a smile she didn't quite feel. "Sure."

Callie watched Colin exit her office, and the moment he disappeared Callie flopped back against her seat. The question remained, how good was she at pulling off the impossible? And how was she going to convince Matt to return to a hands-off relationship?

More important, how was she going to convince herself?

CHAPTER SIX

"THIS REALLY ISN'T necessary, Mr. Croft." Callie pressed the elderly man's handkerchief to the cut on her forehead, hoping the blood had stopped oozing down her face. The E.R. was packed and it was only seven-thirty in the evening. The hour they'd spent in the waiting room so far felt like the tip of the iceberg.

Callie tried again. "It was kind of you to drive me here, but I don't need to see a doctor."

A trickle of blood ran down her hand as she applied pressure to her forehead, and she cursed the timing. How could she convince the man she didn't need medical attention with her arm bringing to mind a horror flick? Served her right for being so distracted.

She'd gone to the costume shop today to rummage around and check out the crucifix she'd spied on the shelf the first day she'd visited the store. Focusing on her work hadn't come easy, especially with the dressing room in her line of sight. And then, while standing on the shelf, she'd received a call from Matt, asking her to dinner.

No wonder she'd dropped the stupid crucifix on her head.

A drop of blood landed on her thigh, and she swiped

the spot with her sleeve before the shop owner noticed. "I'm fine. Really. I can take care of this at home."

The balding man's forehead looked permanently creased with concern. "But that crucifix is heavy. You might need a CAT scan."

That crucifix was heavy, indeed. Hurt like heck on the way down, too. Reaching for the sucker on the top shelf had been a stupid plan. Maybe Matt was right. Maybe she should stick to the cheaper, less authentic, less *heavy* props from here on out. Unfortunately, that didn't solve her problem now. She kept hoping to convince the shop owner to leave, so she could leave, too. When she'd agreed to meet Matt for dinner tonight— to discuss the wedding *only,* she'd stressed to Matt— showing up bleeding wasn't exactly the professional image she'd wanted to project.

A shout from down the hallway caught the attention of the entire waiting room. A man with handcuffs was kicking and screaming and shouting profanities, being escorted by two policemen. One of the cops sported a pretty impressive bloody nose.

Callie sighed and addressed Mr. Croft. "At least go on home to your wife."

So that I can leave this E.R.

"Not until you get checked out by a doctor," Mr. Croft said.

Callie bit back the groan. She hated being forced to go with her last resort but, at this point, she had no choice. She had to call Matt anyway, because making their dinner date looked impossible at this point. And she still hadn't decided how to tell him she was putting their personal relationship, such as it was, on ice.

Callie pulled out her cell phone and placed the call, and Matt answered on the second ring.

"Hey. It's Callie." She turned in her seat to face away from where Mr. Croft was pacing and lowered her voice. "I'm sorry to bother you, but I need your help."

"Does it involve another impossible deal involving sex with our clothes on? Because I'm not sure I'm up for torturing myself tonight."

Despite everything, Callie bit back the smile and went on, "No, nothing like that. I went to Mr. Croft's shop to check out a crucifix for an *Interview with the Vampire* wedding I'm planning."

"Vampires?"

She grinned at the doubtful tone of his voice. "Set to take place at midnight. In a graveyard."

"That's just creepy."

Callie laughed. "Anyway..." She glanced at Mr. Croft, who was now speaking with the clerk again, gesturing anxiously back at Callie.

The poor man was going to have a stroke at the thought of her keeling over from head trauma.

"I reached up to grab the crucifix and managed to knock the thing down on my head." She purposefully didn't share exactly why she'd been so distracted. "And it's, um, a lot heavier than it looks."

"Are you okay?"

"I have a little cut on my forehead. But Mr. Croft is freaking out. I think he's afraid I'm going to keel over and die. He refuses to leave until I get checked out by a doctor."

She could hear the grin in Matt's voice.

"And you just happen to know one," he said.

"I hate asking you for a favor like this. But—"

"Which E.R.?"

"St. Mathews."

"I'm leaving right now."

The next half hour passed by painfully, and Callie was no closer to deciding how to handle Matt. Not only that, the waiting room looked set to explode, every seat full. A couple was arguing and several kids were crying and Callie thought she was going to lose her mind. When the double doors whooshed open and Matt entered, relief swamped Callie, even as awareness shimmied up her spine.

He strode toward her with the look she remembered from the first night they'd met. Focused and intent on solving a problem.

Matt knelt in front of Callie, and she ignored the ridiculous catch in her chest as he lifted the bandage on her forehead, examining the cut.

"How long ago did it happen?" He ran his finger gently down the edge of her tender skin, and she sucked in a breath. The scent of spicy soap hit her nose, and she took in his hair, damp and curling a bit at the edges. Clearly he'd just gotten out of the shower. And the thought of a naked Matt soaping himself made her squirm in her seat.

She'd had the pleasure of having that hard length pressed along her hip...

Mr. Croft appeared beside Callie. "Two hours ago. The crucifix is heavy. I shouldn't have kept it on the top shelf."

Matt sent Callie a conspiratorial wink before assuming a serious face again, looking up at Mr. Croft. "Was there any loss of consciousness?"

"No."

"Any vomiting or slurred speech? Have you noticed her acting or saying anything odd?"

Mr. Croft visibly relaxed a bit. "No."

Good thing the man wasn't privy to her crazy thoughts about Matt.

Matt turned back to Callie. "Feeling dizzy?"

Heck, yeah. Because you're so close, and you smell so good and—oh, my God—those hands.

The feel of his fingers and that hot hazel gaze bringing back the moment on the dock.

"No," she said instead. "No dizziness."

"I don't see a need for a CAT scan." Matt stood, keeping a reassuring hand on Callie's shoulder, and Callie fought the urge to lean into the comforting gesture. "Why don't you let me take her home, Mr. Croft? I can keep an eye on her tonight. If any concerning symptoms crop up, I can bring her back here."

Poor Mr. Croft looked incredibly earnest. Callie could tell the older man wanted to leave, but the worry just wouldn't let him go. "But what about her cut. Shouldn't she get that sutured?"

"The edges are clean." Matt pulled out something shaped like a marker from his pocket, with a clear tip. "We have a special kind of glue we use to close these kinds of lacerations. I can take care of this at home."

"You're sure?"

Matt's face adopted that perfect combination of soothing authority and self-assurance that inspired confidence. "Absolutely."

"Okay. But you'll call if something happens?"

"Of course." Matt sent Mr. Croft a smile that said, "I've got this."

Callie watched the shop owner make his way back

through the automatic doors, not allowing herself to relax until the man disappeared from sight.

She let out a sigh and turned to Matt. "*Thank* you. I thought he'd never leave."

"Guilt." His lips twisted wryly. "The damn emotion is a powerfully motivating force. And, speaking of the emotion, shouldn't you be feeling a little of the same?"

When she looked at him stupidly, he went on.

"You promised a night out on the town, showing me the best that New Orleans has to offer. To make up for the nuclear, skin-melting étouffée I had to eat at your aunt's place. I think I remember something about fine dining. Maybe a little dancing. I believe your condo was mentioned, as well."

Shoot, she'd forgotten all about that. How was she going to get out of this gracefully?

She licked her lips nervously. "Oh, well—"

"I'm only kidding." He gently pulled her to her feet. "A hot night out loses a bit of its appeal when your date is actively hemorrhaging."

"I'm not bleeding anymore." She touched the sore spot with her fingers. "At least not very much."

"How about I get you home, close up that cut and we order takeout?" He cupped her elbow, and she tried to ignore the skin-on-skin contact. "And when you start to vomit profusely, slur your words and your left pupil dilates, I'll call Mr. Croft and tell him I'm dragging you back to the E.R. for a CT scan and emergency brain surgery."

She sent him a sarcastic look.

Matt simply grinned. "Maybe next time you should wait for the proprietor to retrieve the item on the top shelf for you."

"Would you want to watch Mr. Croft crawl up a rickety old ladder?"

"Hmm," he said. "Point taken."

Another shout came up as a State Trooper hauled in a man that appeared to be flying high on something. Sirens wailed outside as an ambulance pulled up to the side ramp. Callie couldn't wait to leave the hectic scenario behind. But Matt? Well, Matt was looking around with an expression of…

Good Lord. Was that *affection?*

"You like the craziness of the E.R., don't you?" she asked.

The little boy grin he sent was adorable. "Love it."

Callie tipped her head. "Does your job in Michigan get this crazy?"

Matt's gaze slid from hers to the overflowing waiting room, the staff bustling about. The chaos in the E.R. appeared to be reaching some sort of zenith. Instead of appearing overwhelmed by the sensory input, Matt looked sorry to be leaving. A nurse came out to announce there was a three-car pileup, with several patients on the way, asking the less urgent patients to please be patient. Matt looked as if he were itching to join in the mayhem and help out.

"Manford E.R. has its moments," he said. "But never anything like this."

So if he didn't stay in Manford for the job, or because he loved the town, why didn't he move? Before she could ask, he linked his fingers with hers, and the contact did crazy things to her pulse. Ridiculous, really, after everything they'd done in the hammock. The simple feel of palm against palm should not be so stimulating.

Matt squeezed her hand lightly. "Time to take you home."

The words zipped through Callie's brain, lighting little fires in their wake. She hesitated. If Matt took her home to fix her cut and keep an eye on her, despite his previous words, the risk of a repeat in the hammock was great.

After informing the clerk to take Callie off the waiting list, they made their way out the door into the night. The air muggy and warm and, after dealing with Mr. Croft for the past hour and a half, Callie had never been so grateful to leave an air-conditioned building. Regrettably, leaving also meant she had to make up her mind how to tell Matt.

And soon.

Thirty minutes later Callie opened the door to her condominium and tried hard not to show just how torn she was by his presence. But she needed to be honest with Matt. No doubt the man expected to finish what they'd started. And, God knows, Callie longed for the same thing.

Just tell him while he cleans up your cut, Callie.

Sure, she'd just wait until he was touching her with those fabulous hands. Nothing wrong with that plan, *at all.*

Her throat tight, Callie set her purse on the foyer table and then led Matt into her kitchen. Matt came to a stop in the middle of the room, scanning the dark wood cabinets, the marble counters and the top-of-the-line kitchen appliances. Despite the small size, her upscale condo had everything she needed, including being located in the fabulous Arts District.

"Not bad for a former tomboy who used to catch crawdads," he said.

Callie smiled. "How about a drink before we get started?"

Lord knows she needed one.

"Scotch?" she asked.

"Absolutely."

Hopefully a bit of alcohol would take the edge off, so she poured two, rehearsing her lines for the conversation that was about to take place.

Handing Matt his drink, she said, "I suppose you heard about Colin and Tommy's big plans to take the DoZ weekend and go public."

Matt sighed and threaded his fingers through his hair, leaving sandy-colored spikes in his wake. "I'm sorry."

She let out a soft huff, amused. "Not your fault."

"You could have said no. Tommy and Penny were already getting what they wanted."

"Colin asked."

Matt said nothing in response, so she handed Matt his drink and he simply followed her down the hall of hardwood floors and into the bathroom containing the same dark wood cabinets and marble counters as the kitchen. The mere fact that Matt hadn't commented meant she had some explaining to do. Callie leaned her hip against the cabinet and watched Matt pull out everything he needed from his bag, totally focused on his task.

She'd experienced firsthand the chaos of the E.R. waiting room. God only knows how much worse the noise and confusion had been in back, which explained a lot about Matt's ability to focus. Obviously the man had learned to block out unnecessary stimuli, concentrating on the task in front of him. And the memory of having all that attention directed at her sent heat crawling up her back.

"I'm curious what kind of hold Colin has over you," Matt said.

"I told you before, I owe him."

"Yeah, but I considered your debt more of an 'I'm going to organize this weekend party for him' kind of obligation. Not an 'I'm going upgrade the whole shindig to a blowout publicity stop' kind of obligation."

He'd stopped, a package of gauze in his hand as he watched Callie closely.

"I'm assuming this has something to do with your college blunder," he went on.

Callie almost laughed at the benign-sounding title he'd given her mistake.

"When I got dragged to the police station, Colin made the long drive to come bail me out. Colin was livid, and I was angry because I hadn't even asked for his help. He just assumed and came." Her voice dropped a notch. "And, unfortunately, the trip wound up screwing up his finals. He…" She looked away for a moment. "He almost flunked that semester."

She took a deep breath, pushing the horrendously shameful memories away. She'd alienated herself from her parents, her boyfriend and most of her friends in one awful day. Not to mention losing the scholarship.

Coming back to New Orleans was the hardest thing she'd ever done, but she didn't regret the move for a moment.

"And now that this weekend has morphed into the party that just won't stop growing, this is a massive opportunity for Rainstorm Games," she said. "And, hence, Colin. The added publicity is also good for my business."

She took a deep breath and met Matt's gaze again, forcing the words out. "I can't pull off doing my job and sorting through—" she gestured her hand between the two of them "—this, whatever *this* is, at the same time."

A hush descended in her bathroom, and the pause felt big enough to swallow her whole. In fact, she kind of wished it would.

Matt set the gauze on the counter and stepped closer, and her awareness of him increased to distracting levels. "You're telling me that you're going to let your guilt keep you from enjoying our time together?"

"It's not guilt."

God, she hated that word. She'd spent the first few years back in New Orleans drowning in a murky sea of remorse. She'd promised herself, *promised,* she'd have nothing more to do with the emotion. But still...

Matt cocked his head and continued to say nothing, and the burn in her belly brought a frown to her mouth.

Damn.

"Okay," she said. "Maybe I do have some leftover guilt."

She hated admitting that to herself, much less to Matt. It was bad enough her parents still brought up her moment of shame, reminding her of all she'd done. She'd been struggling for years to prove to her parents she'd successfully moved on. And how disappointing to realize she'd subjected herself to the same treatment, even if unconsciously done.

Callie sighed and rubbed her forehead. There were

better ways to spend her time than to engage in end-less self-flagellation.

"From what you told me, you're partially responsi-ble for bringing him and his wife together," Matt said. "Shouldn't a happy ending release you from your debt?"

"I can't screw up this wedding and the promotional event—"

"You won't," he said, stepping so close she could see those beautiful flecks in his eyes.

"See?" Heart doing crazy somersaults in her chest, she pressed back against the cabinet. "I can't think when I'm so distracted."

He lifted a hand to her face. "First, I'll be happy to provide lessons on how to remain focused despite dis-tractions. I think the fact that I'm capable of holding this conversation with you...alone...in your condo... a bed just a room away, proves my point. Second, if I promise to let you get plenty of sleep tonight, will that convince you?"

The conflicting desires—the need to prove herself and the need to feel Matt's hands on her again—went to war in her head again. If she cut out all the bare essen-tials, she could do this. Her gaze dropped to the T-shirt stretched across Matt's chest, hugging the lean muscles beneath. How much sleep did one need, anyway?

"I think you sold me when you mentioned the les-sons," she said.

"Good." The sexy smirk on his face just about did her in, and he stepped back. "Just so we're clear, I'm going to clean up your cut and take you to bed. So if you still have a problem with that, you need to let me know now."

How could he say those words so calmly? Especially

with her pulse striving to achieve record rates? The man had stated his plans to take care of her injury and take her to bed, both declarations delivered with the same nonchalant tone as if the two activities were somehow on the same par with each other. She envied his ability to pull the coolly collected demeanor off.

She felt the need to throw him off guard, to keep him on his toes.

"Just so we're *clear*..." Now that the matter had been decided, she pulled off her bloodstained blouse and tossed the garment aside. "Not only did the corset embellish the goods, the push-up bra I wore that day on the dock made me look bigger than I really am."

Holding his gaze, she reached around her back to unfasten her bra, heart thumping hard, record rates achieved. But her pulse shot higher when Matt reached around and gripped her hand, stopping her efforts and putting about an inch of space between their torsos. She stared up at Matt, those beautiful hazel eyes boring into hers. Heat radiated from his body. Or maybe the one generating the scorching temperatures was her.

His voice low, Matt said, "There is absolutely no way I'll be able to take care of that laceration with you bare-chested. So leave the bra on." A muscle in his jaw ticked, and she had the absurd urge to ease the spot with her tongue. "At least until I'm done."

This last was delivered with a light in his eye that could melt metal.

"Nice to know I can at least warrant being labeled a distraction," she said.

"Never fear. You definitely fall into the category of a distraction. A major one. Not only did I bring the necessary equipment to clean and close up the laceration on your forehead, I brought a box of condoms, too, just in case you didn't have any here."

Her heart stopped, and then restarted with a stutter. Unfortunately, the faster rate made concentrating on the conversation difficult. She squirmed and he shot her a mock chastising look.

"You're going to have to be still," he said. "All that wiggling is…distracting."

Callie closed her lids. Best not to stare up into those hazel eyes. "Do you always have trouble focusing when closing up a woman's cut?"

"No, but they are usually dressed in more than a bra." His voice dropped an octave. "And it's never been you before."

His fingers gently traced around the bruised area briefly and she prided herself on her patience. On her ability to keep her eyes closed with that face and those dreamy eyes so close to hers. She felt his breath warm her forehead, and she gripped the counter, fighting the urge to lean up and take that fabulous mouth with hers.

She was too distracted by the memory to worry much about the sound of rustling, as if he were searching for something, but then came a brush of something soft and wet, followed by a sharp sting.

Callie's lids popped open as she sucked in a breath. "My God."

"Sorry."

An antiseptic smell drifted from the cotton ball in his hand, and he leaned in and pressed a kiss close to the wound before pulling his head back.

She stared up at those lips so close. "What are you using to clean the cut? Hydrochloric acid?"

The chuckle that followed brought a wry twist of her lips. "How did you guess?"

Callie studied Matt's face as he gently pinched the skin around the cut and applied the liquid skin adhesive. She concentrated on breathing, the sound of the air conditioner humming, anything to keep herself from rising up on tiptoe to kiss Matt, which wasn't easy. She had firsthand knowledge that he kissed like a dream. He hadn't needed much to bring her to her knees that day on the dock, just his mouth and those fabulous hands.

When he finished, he dropped his hand. "Now, be careful not to open that up until it has time to dry."

"Is that going to interfere with you taking me to bed?"

"Hell, no," he said, and then he covered her mouth with his.

At first it was just a damp press of skin against skin, his mouth slotted against hers. The heat in Callie's belly increased, seeping along her veins, and she rose up on her toes, taking more. With a groan, Matt opened his mouth, forcing Callie's open and tasting her with his tongue. He tipped his head to the right, and then to left, as if comparing how they best fit together. Heart thumping, Callie was just about to pull back and suggest moving things to the bedroom when Matt leaned down, gripped her behind the thighs and lifted her.

Callie pulled her head back. "Wait," she said with a gasp that contained both humor and desire, clutching his shoulders for balance. "What's your plan for providing lessons on how to remain focused despite distractions?"

The crooked smile on Matt's face sent anticipation and heat curling up in her stomach, and she wrapped her legs around his waist. With one hand against her bottom, he supported her weight as he pulled the box of condoms from his bag.

"No worries." He exited the bathroom, heading up the hallway and into her bedroom. He placed her on the bed, staring down at her with a heated look that sent her stomach searching for her toes. "I'll think of something."

His gaze swept down her body, the hazel eyes growing dark, and goose bumps fanned across her skin. Without a word, he pulled off her sandals and stripped her of her clothes, until all that remained were her panties and bra.

She pushed up on one elbow and reached for his shirt. "Let me help."

Matt gently pushed her back down, the crooked smile sinfully sexy. "No," he said. "Wouldn't want you to hurt yourself and pull that head wound back open."

"Then what am I supposed to—?"

Matt gripped her wrists and raised her hands over her head, curling her fingers around the wooden slats of her headboard. He leaned down and pressed a gentle kiss next to her cut.

"Your job is just to hold on and not move," he said.

A stab of desire sliced through her, heating her between the legs. "Not move?" she asked. "But how am I supposed to—"

Matt reached for the button on his shirt, and she watched, mesmerized, as he undid the row of buttons one by one and tossed the shirt aside. His eyes on hers, he reached for the front of his jeans, and Callie's heart picked up its pace. The muscles in his arms and chest rippled as he flicked open his pants and pushed everything down. Lean hips, well-muscled thighs and a heart-attack-inducing erection left Callie struggling to continue the act of breathing.

"Matt…"

The words died as he knelt at her feet, removing her bra and panties. She waited for him to kiss her. Instead, Matt picked up her leg, pressing openmouthed kisses up her shin, her thigh, and then landing on her hip bone.

"The key to keeping that incision safe," he murmured against her skin, "is to remain completely still."

She arched her back, hoping to encourage him to head south. Instead, he trailed higher until his tongue dipped in her navel, sending a skitter of sparks up her spine. He cupped her between the legs and shifted higher, his mouth moving up until it landed on a nipple.

Shock and desire shot through her limbs, and she arched her back, seeking more of that mind-blowing mouth against her skin. Matt circled the tip with his tongue, and Callie sucked in a breath. But just as she was melting at the caress, he ran his tongue down her abdomen, across her hip and landed between her legs.

Heat and pleasure blasted through her. "Oh, my God, Matt," she said, tipping her head back.

When Matt flicked his tongue against her, Callie whimpered, "Please…"

She wanted to wrap her arms around his back and pull his body down. She wanted his naked skin stretched out across the top of hers. She wanted to reach down and clutch his head, pulling him closer.

Fingers tight around the headboard, she said, "Can I let go yet?"

"Nope," he said. At least this time his voice sounded harsh, as if he were wound up tight and needed release.

Jeez, she knew how he felt.

"Not yet," he said.

He sat up on his knees, and Callie's breath escaped with a protesting sound. Palms damp against the wooden slats of the headboard, she watched Matt apply a condom, her fingernails digging into her palms. Eyes homing in on hers, he swooped up her body and buried himself deep between her legs. His pace relentless, he rocked into her.

Mind spinning, muscles straining, she struggled to keep her hold of the headboard as he moved. The intensity in his gaze and the dark, focused look on his face brought her closer to the edge. His body hard, Matt drove her higher, the muscles in his arms lengthening and bulging from his efforts.

"Matt."

"Okay."

His one-word response brought a cry of relief, and Callie wrapped her arms around his back, her legs around his hips, holding him close. Urging him on. Hanging on tight. The heat of pleasure burned hotter, brighter, until Callie was sure she'd burst into flames. Feeling out of control, she gripped his shoulders harder. The orgasm burst outward, shock waves moving through her body, and she closed her eyes, relishing the sensation, barely aware as Matt gave one final thrust, calling out her name.

CHAPTER SEVEN

THE NEXT MORNING, awareness came to Matt in layers, each one better than the one before. Slowly he became cognizant of a comfortable bed, of soft sheets and Callie's hair tickling his cheek, his hand resting on her hip. Her body lay lax, her breathing deep and even as she slept. For a moment he enjoyed the simple pleasure of holding a beautiful woman in his arms. A lazy morning where he had nothing he needed to do and no place he needed to be. Even better?

The potential for a repeat of last night.

He felt more relaxed than he had in a long time and not just because of the sex. Although the activities went a hell of a long way at taking the edge off the tension he'd been carrying around since he'd first laid eyes on Callie. The great sex left his body humming.

A buzzing sound caught his attention, and he peered over Callie's shoulder. His cell phone vibrated madly, inching across the nightstand in its efforts to get his attention. When it went to voice mail, his phone flashed. Five missed calls.

Damn.

Panic punched him, and he bolted upright in bed, picturing Tommy calling for help. The emergency room trying to contact him about his brother being brought in for an overdose. The police calling to deliver the tragic news...

The house was dark when Matt entered—not a peaceful stillness, but the eerie kind that filled him with dread. Suffocating. Terrifying. Anxiety crawled up his spine as he headed up the hallway and called out Tommy's name, getting no answer. He knew his brother was home because his car was in the drive.

When he spied his brother's bedroom door cracked open, Matt's steps slowed, his pulse increased and goose bumps prickled his neck, spreading throughout his limbs. His heart hammered in his chest as he slowly pushed the door open, and certainty slid into place when he saw Tommy lying on the floor, pale, as still as death.

Matt slammed his eyes shut against the memory, nausea rising in his stomach and tightening his chest. How could he have forgotten to check in with Tommy last night?

Matt fought to control his breathing, cursing under his breath, mindful of Callie sleeping next to him. He glanced down. Fortunately, she still appeared to be deep in sleep. Matt rolled out of bed and stood, reaching for the phone. As he scrolled through the missed calls, his heart continued to pound, no matter how much he told himself to calm down.

Every voice message was from Tommy, which meant he wasn't dead. At least not yet.

Relief poured through Matt, and he leaned against the wall, bracing his hands on his knees. Willing himself to friggin' get a grip.

Once he felt steadier, he padded down the hallway

and into Callie's living room. Hitting Tommy's number, Matt collapsed onto the couch and braced for the topic.

Tommy voice sounded worried. "Where the hell have you been?"

Matt rubbed his eyes and let out a self-directed scoff of ridicule.

"Sorry, Tommy. I got distracted."

Matt's mind drifted back to Callie

Yep, very distracted.

Tommy's huff sounded more amused than annoyed. "Yeah, well, when my worrywart of a big brother didn't check in like usual, I got concerned. And with every un-returned call, I thought you'd been mugged and knocked unconscious or something."

The bark of laughter held more bitterness than humor. Hopefully Tommy wouldn't notice.

"Sorry, Tommy. Long story. Wound up making a trip to the E.R. last night."

"You okay?"

"I'm fine. Just…helping out a friend."

"A friend?"

Matt ignored the implied inquiry beneath his brother's tone. "I'm heading back home tomorrow."

His return to Manford was long overdue.

"Good," Tommy said.

The relief in Tommy's voice had Matt sitting up right. For the first time, Matt noticed the tension underlying his brother's voice, a tension that didn't relate to his brother's worries about Matt.

"Are you, uh…?" Being a moron meant Matt's question came out incredibly lame. "Okay?" Matt finished.

Okay, of course, meaning many different things.

Are you sleeping all right?

Having trouble at work?
Using again?

Matt bit back the groan and dropped his head into his hand, phone still pressed to his ear. They'd been skirting the edges of this issue since the last time Matt had picked Tommy up from a thirty-day stint in rehab. And the two years of tiptoeing were tiresome. Because, seriously, how many ways could two men have the same conversation?

If you don't quit, you're going to wind up dead, Tommy.
I've given it up for good, Matt, I swear.

And in Tommy's defense, Matt knew his brother meant the words every time he repeated them.

Tommy's voice brought Matt back to the conversation. "No, everything's fine."

There was an awkward pause. "Good," Matt said, wondering what Tommy was *really* thinking.

"Penny and I will have a couple of steaks on the grill waiting for you when you get off the plane."

As always, Tommy managed to bring a smile to Matt's lips, despite the tension. "Sounds perfect."

Matt signed off and leaned his head back against the couch, closing his eyes. Wishing he could recapture that feel-good, peaceful moment this morning when he'd first woken up. The lingering pleasant buzz from a night of fantastic sex. The lack of the ever-present uneasiness eating away at his stomach. He was too young to feel this damn old.

The residual panic-induced adrenaline still coursed through his limbs. Normally he needed several cups of coffee before being fully awake in the morning. Today, the scare had left him supercharged, and the tension in Tommy's voice still weighed on Matt's mind.

Something had upset his little brother. And if Matt didn't get back soon and get to the bottom of whatever was going on, he might wind up dragging Tommy back to rehab again.

His gut clenched and he felt sick to his stomach.

Jesus, don't throw up.

Callie's voice broke through the unpleasant thought.

"So you're heading out tomorrow?"

Matt opened his eyes and spied Callie leaning in the living-room doorway. She didn't look fully awake, with her honey-colored hair tousled and her eyes sleepy. She was in a T-shirt that just covered her bottom, her long legs bared—legs that had spent a good portion of the night wrapped around him.

Longing surged through him. The urge to pick her up and carry her back to bed was strong.

"Sorry." She pushed the hair out of her face. "I didn't mean to eavesdrop."

"No problem. And, yeah," he said. "I have several shifts I have to work this coming week."

And a brother to check in on.

Callie tipped her head. "Will you be coming back before the wedding?"

Six weeks without seeing Callie again seemed like cruel and unusual punishment. But Matt knew the tightness in his chest wouldn't ease completely with just a quick check on his brother, not with the tension he'd heard in Tommy's voice.

The playful light in Callie's eyes eased the tension until Matt had to fight a smile as he tried to sound serious. "Depends."

Clearly, she caught the underlying tease in his tone. "On what?"

"On whether or not you'll make it worth my while."

"Does a good party hold any merit?" Callie said. "I was hoping you would come to my family reunion with me. You can sit back, relax and enjoy the loaded comments bestowed upon me by some of my relatives. And if that doesn't tempt you—" her lips twisted wryly "—there'll be some great food, too. I just happen to be related to the woman who makes the best shrimp étouffée in two counties. Nice and spicy."

Matt laughed, enjoying the way Callie's dry humor eased that residual tightness in his chest. "That's not the kind of spicy I was hoping for."

Her warm gaze lit with mischief, Callie uncrossed her arms and came closer. And with each step she took every cell in Matt's body became tighter and tighter, focused on the enticing expanse of skin, the tension now of a different sort. And far more welcome.

She came to a stop in front of him. "So will you do a girl a favor and come back for a visit before the wedding?"

Matt looked up at Callie. He'd be crazy to plan a return visit when he had so much on his plate already. Two weeks of work at Manford Memorial, with a four-day stint in one of the busiest emergency rooms in Miami in between. Between travel, the need for sleep and the upcoming wedding, there wouldn't be much in the way of spare time. Adding in an unnecessary trip back to New Orleans clearly bordered on insane.

"I promise you can crash here during your stay," Callie said.

Hell, who could say no to that kind of offer?

Matt gave up, the grin creeping up his face as he

reached for Callie's thigh, pulling her into his lap. "I'll do my best to make it happen."

One week later

At ten o'clock in the evening, Matt let himself into the split-level house he'd grown up in and now shared with Tommy and Penny. Matt tossed his keys on the kitchen counter and rolled his shoulders to ease the tension of a long, boring shift in the E.R. Heading toward his side of the house, he was careful not to wake the sleeping occupants located at the other end. The arrangement had worked out better than he'd originally hoped.

One side of their shared home belonged to Tommy and Penny, providing them plenty of room for privacy. The space contained a bedroom, a family room and a guest-room-turned-gaming-room. The latter had been Tommy's childhood bedroom and, years later, served as his retreat during the worst of his getting-clean stages.

Matt had spent years tiptoeing past the room and hovering outside the closed door, watching and wondering and worrying about Tommy. Even if Tommy had moved out, there was no way Matt could ever enter the room without feeling that sick churn in his stomach, a nausea that always left him longing to vomit, just to purge himself of the feeling. During the worst times, darkness and despair had seemed embedded in every nook and cranny, oozing from the walls and carpet. The lingering echoes of those emotions still pressed in on Matt. Even now he felt the hair rise on the back of his neck every time he glanced up the hallway.

Matt lived on the other side of the house where he

had a bedroom and an office large enough to afford him some private space of his own. The kitchen and living room provided a common area in which Tommy, Penny and Matt could choose to hang out together at the end of the day. Since Matt traveled so much, he rarely spent more than a week at a time at his home base.

Clearly the current living situation wasn't a permanent solution, but for now the arrangement worked. When Penny had joined the Paulson household, Matt had offered to move into one of the nicer apartment complexes up the street. But Tommy had refused to kick Matt out of his home. With Tommy's track record, most of the decent rental properties would refuse to take him on as a tenant. Unfortunately, Penny's history ruled out even some of the shadier places in town. In truth, Matt hadn't fought the setup, mostly because the two couldn't hide much if Matt occasionally occupied the same home.

So they existed in this state of limbo, a lot like the limbo of his and Callie's relationship.

Sighing, Matt entered his bedroom and toed off his shoes. He gripped the hem of his scrub top and wearily pulled it over his head before reaching for his pants. He needed a shower, food and a good night's rest. But mostly, he needed to see Callie again.

Yesterday's sketchy night of sleep had started with dreams of her in a wet T-shirt, Matt's hands roaming freely over the thin cotton, tracing the lace of her bra. As if by magic, then he'd been stroking the bare curves of her breasts. Tasting her skin. Reaching for her shorts. And because everything came easy in a dream, suddenly she'd been naked, squirming beneath him with an endless amount of enticingly silky skin, and he'd been licking his way down her flat stomach and to her inner thigh...

He needed to get a grip.

Last week's flight back home had been delayed and he'd been stuck in the Minneapolis airport for twelve hours and, instead of catching a much-needed nap, he'd spent the entire time fantasizing about being back in Callie's bed. Not exactly the way to encourage grabbing some shut-eye on the plane, either. By the time he'd arrived home in Michigan, it was almost 3:00 a.m. and he was dead-tired, frustrated and ready to turn around and head back to New Orleans. Instead, he'd dropped into bed and tossed and turned, missing Callie even more. He'd finally fallen into an exhausted sleep and slept until nine in the morning, which meant he'd missed seeing Tommy before his brother left for work.

An anxious twist in Matt's chest had him clutching his dirty clothes, and he dumped his scrubs into the wicker hamper with more force than necessary.

At first glance, everything had seemed fine at home. Tommy looked good, Penny looked good and both appeared to be continuing on the path of the straight and narrow. Dinner that first night together had included steaks on the grill, as promised, but Tommy's behavior seemed off. The nagging feeling wasn't anything Matt could put a decisive finger on. There was a distance Matt wasn't used to, especially since they'd been living in each other's pockets for the past two years. And the tension had now been gnawing at Matt's insides for days.

Matt pondered the possible causes as he showered

and dressed in sweatpants and a T-shirt. He padded into the kitchen. Standing at the kitchen counter, he ate delicious leftover pasta, thanks to Penny, who knew how to cook. Adding her to the mix had definitely improved the cuisine in the Paulson house.

Two of his three requirements met, and with sex with Callie disappointingly out of the question, he knew sleep was still a long way off. Matt headed for his office and dropped onto the leather couch, turning on his laptop on the coffee table.

An icon popped on his screen, indicating Callie had just flipped on her computer. With her a time zone behind him, the late hour wasn't quite as bad for her as for him. He hesitated for a moment and then hit the call button.

The moment Callie's image appeared on screen, he felt his tension ease. She was sitting cross-legged on her bed, wearing pajamas. Unfortunately, the fifteen-inch screen on his laptop didn't do her beautiful eyes justice.

"This is a surprise," she said.

"A pleasant one, I hope."

"Absolutely."

He couldn't see the playful light in her gaze, but he knew of its presence because of her tone. And for a moment, all he wanted was to climb onto a plane and fly back to New Orleans where everything seemed so much easier and simpler.

And certainly a hell of a lot more fun.

"Did I interrupt anything?" he asked.

"Nothing exciting."

Files and small patches of fabric samples surrounded Callie on the bed. A silk robe clung to her shoulders but remained open in front. Matt spied a lacy tank top and what looked like a feminine pair of…

"Are those boxer shorts?" he said.

"You can take the tomboy out of the country, you know, but…" Smiling, she finished the sentence with a shrug and reached for her bedside table, picking up a glass of white wine. "At least they're hot pink and edged with lace. Besides, I haven't had to entertain company this late at night since you left."

A twinge of possessiveness flared, and Matt tamped it down and concentrated instead on the twinkle in her eyes on the monitor.

Her hair hung in a gentle loop at the nape of her neck, gathered in some sort of casual twist that managed to look comfortable and pretty and sexy, all at the same time. An empty plate on her nightstand suggested she'd just finished her dinner. Clearly she'd eaten in bed.

He wished he'd eaten in her bed, too.

Matt glanced at the files scattered on her comforter. "What are you working on?"

Her smile held more than a hint of mischievousness. "Just sitting down to compose my reply to an *Ex Factor* reader for my blog. Actually, you're the perfect person to help me with my response."

Matt let out a soft scoff. "I doubt that. I thought this was Colin's department."

Callie laughed. "He's responsible for the man's view, yes. But I wanted your thoughts before I replied."

"What's the question?"

Two seconds ticked by before she answered.

"A bride-to-be asking for advice on how to convince her future brother-in-law to walk her down the aisle," she said.

The one-two punch to his conscience came out of the blue, shocking the hell out of him.

Matt let out a groan. "You're making that up."

Callie shifted some paperwork and fabric swatches aside, settling back against her headboard with her glass of wine in hand. She stretched those toned, silky legs in front of her, bringing to mind when they'd been wrapped around his waist. The inside of his chest grew hot, heating the blood shooting through his veins.

When would he get a chance to hold her again?

He pushed the hopeless thought aside and concentrated on Callie, who was currently eyeing him over the rim of her wineglass. An expression like that meant trouble for sure.

She took a sip and carefully set her drink on the nightstand. "I had a long talk with Penny yesterday."

Of course she had.

"She was desperately trying to come up with someone to walk her down the aisle," Callie said. "And I told her she should ask you again."

Matt shifted uneasily on the couch, propping his feet on the coffee table just to the left of his laptop. Might as well get comfortable for the conversation ahead.

"Yeah?" he replied in his best noncommittal voice.

He knew Tommy was disappointed Matt hadn't told Penny he'd give her away. His brother hadn't come out and said as much, but Matt knew. The closer they drew to the date of the wedding, the tenser things had grown. Still, compared to all the other issues brewing between them, Penny's request seemed minor in comparison.

Callie's lighthearted tone was long gone. "Matt, you said yourself that I should be grateful for the family I have. That I should get over myself and go to that reunion because wasting the family I have was stupid."

His brow crinkled. "Those are *not* the words I used."

"No," she said, her chuckle drifting over the speaker. "You were definitely more tactful. But that's what you meant. And you were right. Going to the reunion is the right thing for me to do. I have a family. One that wants to see me, even if they do make the occasional callous remark." Callie sat up a touch, her brown eyes earnest, her voice soft. "You don't have that choice because your parents are dead, and that's a tragedy. But Penny doesn't have a choice, either. Her parents refuse to have anything to do with her." She paused before going on. "And that's a tragedy, too."

"I know."

Several beats passed by before Callie went on, tipping her head. "Do you not like Penny?"

He resisted the urge to bring the video chat to a close. He could sign off and close the lid to the laptop and be done with this conversation. But no matter the topic, the sight of Callie in her sexy boxer pj's was impossible to resist.

"It's not that." Matt wearily scrubbed his hand down his face. "Penny's fine."

And he meant the words, he seriously did. They weren't just a platitude he pulled out of his ass when convenient. He admired anyone who could fight an addiction and win. He knew better than most just how hard that battle could be. Penny was bright, capable and, if nothing else, she clearly loved Tommy.

"Are you against this marriage?" Callie asked.

"No." He winced at the force behind his words. He

dropped his hands into his lap, and his voice dropped several octaves, as well. "Maybe."

In response to Callie's hiked brow, Matt let out a sigh. "Yes."

Despite the harsh word, it felt good to get the sentiment off his chest. From the very moment Tommy had introduced Penny to Matt, Matt had been fighting the part of him dying to find a way to send the woman packing. He let out a soft scoff at the thought. As if he held *that* kind of power in his hands.

But the overwhelming urge had nothing to do with Penny personally and *everything* to do with the need to protect his brother, no matter what.

Matt felt like a dirtbag for admitting he didn't want Tommy and Penny to marry, but Callie's gaze remained free of judgment. And as he studied those beautiful brown eyes, relief slowly washed over him because he knew he could be absolutely, brutally honest with Callie. No matter how ugly his feelings, she wouldn't hate him for the truth.

He definitely could have used her steady presence during the worst of Tommy's addiction years.

"Tell me," she said softly.

The tight knot in his chest unwound a bit. "Jesus, Callie," he groaned out. "It's like taking the potential for disaster and multiplying the bloody thing by a hundred."

"What are you talking about?"

He dragged a hand through his damp hair, knowing he was leaving tufts sticking out in all directions. "I'm talking about Tommy relapsing and dragging Penny down with him." He scowled in an attempt to mask the all-consuming fear as he considered the alternative.

"Or vice versa. If she starts using again, how is Tommy going to resist temptation?"

Fear gripped him, and he hated himself for succumbing to the familiar emotion.

He shifted on the couch again. Now that he was on a roll, the words spilled out. "Or let's say they do manage to stay clean while they're together. What happens if the relationship tanks? Because let's face the facts here. Two former users probably aren't the most stable of sorts. How would Tommy handle the stress of a breakup and not be tempted to slip?"

Callie pursed her lips in thought as she reached for her glass and took another sip of wine. "Every relationship has the potential to tear a person down." She set her drink aside and met Matt's gaze again. "And this one is no different."

He briefly pressed his lids closed, wishing the logic helped. "I know."

But how many ran the potential to lead to something so dark? So permanent? Because nothing was more permanent than *death*.

Callie crossed her arms across her chest. "Tommy and Penny understand each other better than anyone else ever could. Yes, they could bring each other down. There's no doubt about that." She didn't sugarcoat the words, even allowing more time for them to sink deep before going on. "But I happen to believe they'll hold each other up."

He hiked a brow dryly. "Yeah, well, you arrange weddings for a living. Your favorite character is Elizabeth Bennet, a woman who conveniently managed to fall in love with a man who could save her family from destitution. A fairy tale."

"*Pride and Prejudice* is not a fairy tale."

Matt hiked a brow. "Close enough. Seriously, Callie, real life rarely works out like that." He let out a self-directed scoff. "You see happily ever after around every corner, but I get to patch people up after they beat the crap out of each other."

I get to be the lone family member left to pull my brother out of the gutter, over and over again.

"Did you have a bad shift tonight?" she asked.

Hell, yeah.

"Kind of," he said instead. Despite the topic of conversation, Matt fought a smile, his lips twitching at the memory. "The chief of staff argued with the head of E.R. about transferring a patient, a divorcing couple had a screaming match in triage and two best friends showed up because they'd beat the crap out of each other over a computer game."

Callie rolled her eyes. "The friends were guys, I'm assuming."

"Yeah. It started out as a joke and ended up fairly ugly," Matt said. "To be fair, a case of beer had been consumed, so I'm not sure you can hold them completely accountable for their stupidity."

"Of course you can hold them accountable," she said. "There's no excuse for being stupid enough to drink so much alcohol that a computer game becomes more important than a friendship."

Callie leaned forward and came closer to the screen, lying on her belly and folding her arms on the bed. The new position brought her close enough for him to see the light in her eyes. This time the spark was earnest, nothing playful about it at all.

"Penny needs you right now, Matt. She's going to be

a sister of sorts, and you owe it to your brother to start this relationship out on the right foot." A line appeared between her brows. "Don't make Penny keep paying for the same mistakes over and over again."

Callie was right. He *knew* she was right. Penny and Tommy both deserved Matt's unconditional support. But so far, he'd let fear rule his reactions. The habit would be difficult to break because the fear ran so deep that nothing short of a scalpel could cut the sucker out, and even that would take a significant piece of Matt during the process.

He'd just have to carry on with the fear firmly in place.

Matt blew out a breath and studied the woman on the screen, wishing like hell they were in the same room. "Man, I wish I could touch you right now."

A glimmer appeared in her eyes. "Tell you what," she said. "If you agree to at least have a conversation with Penny about the wedding, I'll let you watch me touch myself."

The bark of shocked amusement slipped out even as Matt's heart set up a pounding pace beneath his sternum. "Are you freaking kidding me?"

"I'm deadly serious."

He eyed Callie's cleavage, the potential blooming and bringing all sort of delicious scenarios to mind. "How many glasses of wine have you had?"

"I just had a conversation with my mother," she said dryly, "which rarely goes well. The numbing effects of two glasses of wine are about the only way I can survive our conversations. Unfortunately, that's just enough alcohol to also make me reckless—" a huge grin crept up her mouth "—but not enough to excuse me from my stupidity."

Callie dropped the robe down her shoulders and tossed it aside, leaving her lacy tank and the curve of her breasts displayed. The view on Matt's screen improved considerably.

"I'll touch mine if you'll touch yours," she said smoothly.

The libido-punching words and the seductive look on her face morphed his blood into flaming rivers of fire, licking along his limbs. He fisted his hand, fighting the groan.

He'd give anything to able to reach through the screen and pull Callie onto his lap. His mind filled with images of his time with Callie: the wet shirt plastered against firm breasts, her cheeks flushed, her mouth parted as she convulsed around his fingers in the hammock.

Even better? Callie beneath him as she'd urged him on in her bed.

On screen, she reached for the hem of her lacy tank and pulled the fabric over her head.

Callie now sat there, beautiful breasts exposed, her top dangling from her finger. "So what do you think?"

His voice hoarse, he said, "I think what they say about cameras is right."

"What do they say?" she said as she tipped her head curiously, a lock of honey-colored hair falling across her cheek.

And a bare-chested woman had no right looking so innocently adorable and sexy and sophisticated, all at the same time.

"The lens does add five pounds." A teasing grin tried

to hijack his mouth. "Specifically, 2.5 to each side. You look bigger, even without the corset."

She threw back her head and laughed, and the sound soothed away the lingering bits of his bad mood, courtesy of a shift with patients who'd brought their arguments into his E.R. Matt's muscles relaxed as the tension slipped away.

Callie scooted forward and propped her elbows on the bed, her breasts now hanging in full view of the camera. The immediate reaction of Matt's libido almost did him in, tenting his sweatpants in an embarrassing way, and he tried to discreetly ease the pressure by tugging on his waistband.

"Careful," Callie said, "or I'll hit the minimize tab on the screen, and you'll look much smaller."

A hoarse chuckle escaped. "Don't you dare."

Though God knows he had bigger worries to be concerned about, like the fact that moving air in and out of his chest suddenly felt complicated.

"I haven't been sleeping well." Her tone husky, she slowly slid a hand down her stomach. "You?"

His voice felt raw. "No."

"If you agree to talk to Penny, I'll let you watch me masturbate."

His already straining erection strained some more, and his groin grew so tight he thought he'd crack in half, Christ, every muscle was tensed and ready and willing and able, urging Matt to do exactly whatever Callie asked.

But wouldn't he be better off calling a halt to this impossible relationship now? Every interaction led him further and further down a slippery slope. He'd shown up in New Orleans to find a wedding planner and leave, but had wound up staying for two weeks. He'd left for home with the plan of returning for the wedding, and moved heaven and earth to free up some time for another trip back. Until eventually breaking things off felt impossible.

"And then I can watch you do the same," she said.

"You want me to masturbate on camera for you?"

"Why not?" she said. "We're both grown-ups. If I sign off now, what will you do?"

"Take care of this myself."

"What's a little video sexting other than a way to challenge ourselves? You know, up the ante on our third-base event on the dock."

"So now, instead of third base we're...what?" He quirked a teasing eyebrow. "Hitting zero base?"

"You wouldn't want to deprive me of the pleasure of watching, would you?"

Desire shot through his limbs, his heart slamming in his chest, and he tugged on the leg of his briefs, dying to provide a little relief.

"Why are you so intent on this little endeavor, anyway?" he asked.

"You look like you've had a crappy day."

"I did."

The arguing of the administrators had been prolonged and, as with most management types, full of a lot of hot air as both sides seemed intent on hearing themselves speak. Matt just wanted to provide appropriate care for the patient. But the scene had morphed into Matt being thrown into the mix of two men running for political office. And between the fighting friends and the divorcing couple, the evening had ended on a truly sucky note.

A little sexual release seemed a small pleasure to ask.

But part of him wondered about the point of this little, well, *exercise,* for lack of a better word. Callie lived in New Orleans. Callie *loved* New Orleans. And her business clearly thrived in a city that provided ample opportunity for themed weddings. Matt knew few couples, if any, would travel to Manford, Michigan, to fulfill their adventure wedding fantasies. And he certainly couldn't move because Tommy lived here.

The last time Matt had left his little brother for too long, Tommy had almost died….

Matt slammed his eyes closed, torn between what he wanted now and what he feared would be too hard to let go of later.

"Matt."

He opened his eyes and found Callie had shifted on her bed.

"Okay," he said. "I can't promise anything, but I'll think about having a conversation with Penny."

"That's all a girl can ask," Callie said.

A palm cupped her breast and her seeking hand finally slid beneath the front of her boxers. "I have a thing for your broad shoulders," she murmured. "I have ever since the dressing room." Her honey words rolled over him, and her thumb began to circle the tip of her breast. "I love the feel of your hard chest against mine when you move on top of me." The bud hardened and swelled, and blood *whooshed* annoyingly in his ears. He didn't want to miss even the tiniest inflection in the drawl.

Her eyes glazed over. "Picture me spread beneath you."

His chest struggled to suck in enough oxygen.

She looked like every adolescent's wet dream.

Granted, she didn't have as lush a figure as most centerfolds. But he craved the feel of her skin, her taste on his tongue and the toned legs. The gentle flare of her hips was just enough to entice a man. Her breasts were perfectly formed. As her breath came faster, the tips rose and fell faster with every breath. The hand down her panties moved faster. The fact that he couldn't see exactly what was going on was almost hotter for the secrecy.

The only thing he knew for certain was that she was ready for him. If he was in her bed right now, he could pull her beneath him and thrust deep, no foreplay needed. Good God, he closed his eyes and remembered sliding between those silken thighs and into her wet heat.

With a groan, he reached into his pants and grasped his erection. He ignored the thoughts swirling in his head as he began to stroke himself.

"Matt—" Callie's voice cracked.

"I know."

"Hurry," she said.

His hand pumped a little harder as he watched her eyes glaze over, her hips start to roll with every movement of the hand between her legs. He grew so tight he thought he'd crack.

"That's really..." Her voice trailed off. She sounded out of breath. "Hot," she drawled.

"Is *hot* the agreed upon safe word?"

"Do we need a safe word?"

"With you around, hell, yeah."

Nothing was safe with Callie around, most of all his sanity.

Even on screen he could see the flush on her cheeks

and her lips part as she began to pant for breath. And while his gaze remained locked on hers, every once in a while he saw her tick her gaze down. To watch what he was doing.

Frustrated by the constricting fabric, Matt gave up on restraint and tugged his sweatpants down to his thighs before returning his hand to his erection, his hand beginning an intense rhythm. His attention drifted between memories of Callie moving beneath him in bed and the live picture of her on screen. Sweat dotted his upper lip, and the pleasure wound tighter. He remembered the scent of her shampoo and the sounds she made as she clutched his back. Callie whimpered—even that tiny sound held a hint of the South. A second ticked by before he realized the noise had come from Callie and not just his memories.

"Oh, my God, Matt. I can't—" Callie's voice gave out.

He glanced at her, and suddenly Matt couldn't suck in the oxygen fast enough.

Matt had the overwhelming urge to lean forward and lick the computer screen, a sad substitute for the sweet taste of Callie's skin. Instead, he imagined taking her nipple into his mouth and sucking hard, picturing her writhing against him. He could almost smell the scent of sex, the feel of sweat-slicked skin against sweat-slicked skin. An electric energy pulsed in his groin, demanding to be released.

Don't you dare finish first, Paulson.

"Callie," he whispered, his voice hoarse.

The single, desperate word had the intended effect. Callie arched her back and let out a long, low moan.

Despite the soft tone, the sound slammed into Matt, and he closed his eyes, following on her heels.

Matt had no idea how much time ticked by before he could focus again. Slowly he became aware of his heaving breaths, and he lifted his head to stare at the computer screen. Callie had a dreamy look on her face and a slight smile on her lips.

"Hey," she said softly.

"Hey, yourself."

Her smile grew bigger. "Aren't you glad you agreed?"

A chuckle escaped. "Callie, hitting zero base with you is a hundred times better than hitting a home run with someone else."

CHAPTER EIGHT

CALLIE WEAVED HER way through the crowded baggage terminal of the Louis Armstrong New Orleans International Airport, dodging passengers and carts loaded with luggage as she looked for Matt. Because of the location of the airport and her condo in relation to her family reunion, he'd insisted on taking a taxi to her place because picking him up would have been out of her way. And they'd be cutting the timing close enough.

She'd finally pretended to give in. But surprising him as he gathered his bags had been her plan all along. Because Matt had decided to make the trip back to New Orleans again. A special trip, just to see her. And she had every intention of making the most of the three-day weekend.

She knew how hard he'd worked to clear his schedule so he could come back for her family reunion. The effort he'd exerted on her behalf generated a lovely feel-good buzz, along with an anticipation and hope that left her alarmed at her own stupidity.

Don't expect too much, Callie.

She shoved back the warning voices in her head, promising herself not to think negative thoughts. Matt hadn't gone out of his way to steal an extra couple of days with her just so she could wallow in doubt about the future. She spied a broad back and sandy hair that curled a little at the collar, and pleasure flushed up her back.

Nope, not a chance. She intended to enjoy every second they spent together.

She grinned as she tapped one side of a very nice set of shoulders. "Excuse me, sir. Do you have the time?"

Matt turned, and, if she'd been holding out for a smile, she'd have been disappointed.

Instead of responding, he hooked his hand behind her neck and dragged her close, her body crash-landing into his. He kissed her without apology, nothing tentative or hesitant about the maneuver. Hot and hungry and brimming with heat, his hard lips moved across hers as if he'd been thinking of nothing else for the entire flight down. Perhaps since last night.

Maybe for the past two weeks.

Callie gripped his shirt and pulled him close, moaning into his mouth as she plastered her torso tighter against his. She met him turn for turn, taste for taste. Despite the crowd, she did her best to show him she'd missed him, too. His tongue rasped against hers, want and need and determination stamped in his every action. Like a gentle assault she couldn't quite fend off, not that she had any desire to do such a ridiculous thing.

When the need to inhale grew too great, Callie pulled back.

"Though my appreciation for Skype has skyrocketed, I much prefer face-to-face encounters." Matt grinned and looked down the front of her blouse, no doubt seeing the lacy cups of her push-up bra. "You hiding a watch down there?"

"Nope." She held up her wrist. "Today I'm wearing one like everybody else."

His lips quirked. "How disappointing."

"No worries," she said, mimicking his favorite phrase. "I'll make it up to you later."

"You mean after I eat lunch with the LaBeau family and start sweating cayenne pepper out of my pores?"

Callie laughed. "I can't wait." Though the thought of the entire LaBeau family being present left her nibbling on her lip in concern. All those aunts and uncles and cousins she hadn't seen in so long, swarming around her...

The day had started out cloudy and cool and stayed so for most of their two-hour drive. Fortunately, the sun finally broke through the clouds just in time for Callie to arrive at the outdoor park by the Mississippi River, Matt by her side. The crowd of LaBeaus had already gathered around the tables set up lengthwise, enough food to feed the town of New Orleans, and then some.

Callie eyed the crowd, a swell of nausea slaying the last of her appetite. "I'm thinking we should do this in small doses."

He frowned in confusion. "You mean eat?"

"No," she said. "Meet my relatives."

"If I can survive Aunt Billie's étouffée then I can definitely handle your relatives."

"Oh, they'll love you." Callie's smile felt tight. "It's me they might have a problem with."

Aunt Billie stopped by first, and Callie was grateful her aunt was so reliable. A few teasing comments later, and Callie knew she was blushing, and then a warm welcome for Matt was delivered with a hug and an offer to bring him some of her étouffée herself. Promising, of course, to bring him the milder version this time.

The next thirty minutes passed uneventfully. A few aunts and uncles and distant cousins wandered by, not to mention a few people she couldn't pin down her relationship to. Callie made the introductions and there were a few wayward comments about how long it'd been since she last came to the reunion. Several questions about her business, and one or two that were an indirect reference to her past. All in all, mostly just a whole lot of chitchat that didn't mean much. But, in some ways, meant *everything.* Slowly, her tension eased to bearable levels, and she stopped bracing every time another family member approached.

And then her parents arrived.

Callie watched her mother make her way across the grass in Callie's direction. They had the same figure, except her mother's hips reflected her love of the homemade biscuits she had perfected years ago.

"Hey, Mama."

She leaned in to kiss her mother on the cheek, even as dread curled up in her stomach and took up more than its fair share of room.

"I just heard about the weekend event you're arranging for Colin," her mother said. "A friend of mine heard about it on the radio."

Callie bit back the sigh and plastered a smile on her face. "Actually, I'm arranging the weekend for a *client,* Mama." She gestured at Matt, grateful for his steady presence at her side. "Matt Paulson hired me to help with his brother's wedding. Tommy and his fiancée met online playing one of Colin's games."

"What a lovely story," her mother said with a nod at Matt.

The way her mom eyed him made it clear she couldn't care less about the engaged couple. The brother of the groom, on the other hand...

"Callie's doing an excellent job," Matt said.

"I'm sure she is," her mother said. She turned to look at Callie. "Your little party business does seem to be doing quite well."

Your little party business...

Her mother always qualified Callie's business in such a way as to make her feelings known. As if being a themed wedding planner was okay, but only if you had no other options.

Callie's heart slipped lower in her chest as her face strained to maintain the smile, and she ignored Matt's gaze as his brows tented curiously over his eyes. He opened his mouth as if to say something, and then pressed his lips into a firm line. Apparently, in five seconds Matt had surmised the best way to deal with Callie's mother.

The proverbial biting of the tongue.

Though Callie wished she was biting his instead.

Heaven help her, not the thought to be having while holding a tricky conversation with her mother. Matt reached out and settled his hand in the small of her back, and Callie sent him a grateful look. The smile he responded with calmed her nerves and she returned the smile.

"Callie is quite bright," her mother said to Matt before turning back to Callie. "Imagine what you could have done if you'd applied the same energy to a law practice."

Her heart slipped to her toes. She knew how proud her parents had been when, in high school, she'd announced she wanted to go to law school. They'd proudly shared the news every time they'd gone back to visit their old hometown. There wasn't a single relative, distant or otherwise, that hadn't been invested in her progress at college.

And then she'd gotten arrested and lost her scholarship and…

Dear God.

Callie tried to come up with a response. "Mama—"

But that was it, because what else was there to say?

"She's the best themed wedding planner in New Orleans," Matt said smoothly.

Jeez, why was she standing here so tongue-tied? She should say something to her mother. She should defend her business, her life, her *choices.* Instead, she let Matt come to her defense.

"Of course she's the best," Callie's mother said. "But there really isn't that much competition." She tipped her head and met Matt's gaze. "Are you two dating?"

Callie's heart attempted to leap from her chest and she lightly gripped her mother's elbow. *"Mama."*

"What?" Belle LaBeau said, as if she didn't understand why Callie was so upset.

Callie shot Matt an apologetic smile. "Matt, will you excuse us for a moment please?"

The amusement twinkled in Matt's eyes. "No worries."

Callie began to drag her mother in the direction of a flat, grassy spot overlooking the river.

"Mama," Callie said, careful to keep her voice low. "What are you doing?"

"When my daughter brings a man to our family reunion, I have to assume he's more than just a client."

"Matt is—" Callie wearily swept her hair from her face. "He's not—" She dropped her hand to her side, frustrated by her inability to identify what Matt was, not only to her mother, but to herself, as well. "He's just…a friend."

Good Lord. She'd been reduced to a lying, babbling idiot.

"Does Matt live in New Orleans?" her mother asked.

The question landed like a well-placed barb in Callie's gut. What was it about mothers that gave them the ability to sniff out the painful heart of a matter in 3.3 seconds flat?

"No," Callie said, and her face felt like it would crack from the effort to keep from frowning. "He lives in Manford, Michigan."

"Never heard of it," Belle said.

"Neither had I before meeting Matt," Callie said.

"Does he have family around these parts?"

"No," Callie said, gritting her teeth.

"No ties to New Orleans at all?"

"None whatsoever, Mama."

The longer the back and forth went, the more tense Callie's spine became, until she'd thought she'd snap in half. The fact her mother was verbalizing Callie's secret concerns only made matters worse.

Thankfully, Callie's mother paused. But before Callie's tight muscles could lessen even a smidgen, Belle LaBeau opened her mouth to speak again, and Callie interrupted her.

"Is this really necessary, Mama?"

When they reached the far end of the grassy spot, Callie let go of her mother's arm.

"It's just a simple question, Callie. Surely Mr. Paulson doesn't mind? You two are either dating, or you're not." She hiked a brow. "So?"

Callie opened her mouth. "I—"

Belle LaBeau's brow shifted even higher.

"I don't know," Callie finished in a rush.

The disappointment in her mother's eyes was a familiar look. "Callie," she said with a defeated tone. "When are you going to do more than arrange *other* people's weddings and find a man of your own?"

And with that, her mother pivoted on her heel and headed back to the pack of relatives in the park. Callie stared after her.

Are you two dating?

How come she didn't have an answer to her mother's question? But there were also more important questions at hand. The wedding weekend was coming up quickly, and once the event was over, what would happen then?

Matt swung the handle with everything he had, and the ax rotated through the air and struck the wood with a solid *whump,* well outside his intended target. The small crowd gathered around the booth moaned in sympathy. Matt propped his fist on his hip, frowning at the bright red bull's-eye, the blade buried a good two feet from the outside ring.

Clearly he wouldn't be winning any awards today.

"Good thing you have other skills to recommend you, because I'm not sure you'd do so well in the Middle Ages."

At the sound of Callie's voice from behind, Matt smiled and turned to face her.

Dressed in a simple medieval barmaid dress, Callie grinned up at him. Friday had been pure chaos as the wedding guests who'd arrived early at the designated hotel had gathered for dinner at a local restaurant. Matt's time with Callie had been disappointingly limited since he'd arrived in town for the wedding, too much of Callie's days taken up with last-minute details or impromptu meetings with Penny and Tommy.

And Matt refused to be amused by the sight of Callie's and Tommy's heads bowed together, both getting excited over some ridiculous detail about the weekend. Last evening he'd caught the two of them huddled together in a corner, engaged in an earnest debate about how to set up the ax-throwing competition so as many people as possible could enjoy the view.

Unfortunately, at the time, Matt had had no idea this would be to his disadvantage.

"I think I just lost the first round," he said as he headed for Callie.

She smiled and stepped closer, closing the gap between them. "You need someone to cheer you up?"

Matt linked his fingers with hers and led Callie a few steps away, pulling her beneath the awning of a neighboring tent that wasn't quite as crowded and offered a bit of privacy. Fortunately the heat wave had ended long ago, and while the skies were clear and sunny, the cool breeze meant Matt wouldn't be needed to treat the participants for heat stroke.

A definite plus in his book.

Grateful for the rare moment alone, he leaned in to nuzzle Callie's ear, enjoying the scent. Her hair smelled of magnolias and her skin smelled like…well, like *Callie*. And how he recognized the scent after only two months, with only two actual weeks together, was beyond him.

"Cheer me up? What did you have in mind?" he said.

Callie placed her hand on his chest and leaned in close. "I'll tell you tonight if you stop by my place before heading back to the hotel."

"I could skip going back to my hotel room altogether."

"You could. However, if you spend *all* night at my place I won't be at my best tomorrow."

"So?"

He kissed his way up her neck and lightly nipped the delicate shell of her ear before stealing a hard kiss. But the simple contact felt majorly insufficient. He returned to delve deeper, tasting her tongue with his, enjoying the way she gripped the hair at his neck, as if needing the stability to stay upright.

"Just how much sleep do you need in order to pull tomorrow off, anyway?" Matt asked against her mouth.

"I'm not sure," she whispered back.

The sound of a throat clearing broke the spell.

Matt looked up and found Tommy staring at them both with the hugest grin on his face, his arm wrapped around Penny. With her black, pixie cut hair and petite frame, she looked fragile enough to break. That she'd survived what she'd done to her body never ceased to amaze Matt. Tommy was taller than Matt by an inch, but thinner by twenty pounds. At least he no longer appeared gaunt. Neither one looked as if they were nervous about the wedding tomorrow. In fact, in their medieval outfits they looked like just two of the guests enjoying the day.

Tommy's gaze shifted from Matt to Callie and then back again. "Can I steal Callie for a second, Matt?"

Matt fought like hell to pretend that heat wasn't rising up his face at his little brother catching him necking like a stupid schoolkid. Tommy looked intensely amused, if not a little shocked. Not surprising given Matt hadn't been forthcoming about his relationship with Callie. Mostly because he knew there would be questions. Questions he didn't know how to respond to.

Questions he didn't know the answer to himself.

Matt's voice came out gruffer than he'd planned. "No problem. Have at it. I'm sure you both have stuff to discuss about tomorrow."

Callie didn't look embarrassed at all. Instead, she seemed to find something in Matt's face humorous.

She reached up to plant a kiss on his lips. "I'll meet you at the LARP tent at two?"

"Sure."

Tommy and Callie instantly launched into a debate about a problem with this afternoon's schedule for the live-action role-playing as they headed in the direction of the LARP tent. Penny turned to look up at Matt, and he felt her gray gaze all the way to his medieval-approved work boots.

Wasn't dealing with a kid brother enough? Must he endure his soon-to-be sister-in-law's amusement, too?

But Penny's eyes were somber as she looked at Matt. "I want to thank you again for agreeing to walk me down the aisle."

Matt bit back a groan and shifted on his feet. He'd almost prefer being mocked for acting like a schoolkid who couldn't keep his hands to himself. When he'd decided to tell Penny he'd changed his mind, he chose to make the announcement with as little fanfare as possible. So two nights after his conversation with Callie, and the spectacular Skype call, Matt had mentioned at dinner that he'd be fine with walking Penny down the aisle, if she still wanted him to.

Tommy had looked speechless, and Penny had barely managed to let out a shocked yes before Matt had picked up his plate and concentrated on the cleanup. Too bad he didn't have any pressing activities he could bury himself in now. Somehow, he didn't think signing up for a second try at ax-throwing qualified as pressing.

Especially given his hideous lack of skills.

He swept his gaze across the field of white tents, the setting like the base encampment prior to one of the many epic battles in *The Lord of the Rings*. A crowd of people milled about in their costumes. But, unfortunately, nothing required Matt's immediate attention.

He aimed for a nonchalant shrug, hoping he pulled it off. "No biggie."

Penny let out a small laugh, but Matt got the impression that there was zero humor in the act. "It's a very big deal for me. I mean, I know I'm not exactly the girl you had in mind for Tommy."

Despite everything, Matt let out an amused scoff. "That's assuming I even gave the matter much thought. I was too busy trying to keep him alive."

He hadn't meant to let the last bit slip out.

"I know you were." She stepped forward and laid a hand on Matt's arm. "I love him, Matt. I really do."

Oh, God. How had he suddenly become the trusted

sidekick in a chick-flick movie, slated as the confidant he never wanted to be? Ever. In this life, or the next.

"I know how close you two are, and I just wanted to say..." her lips twisted, and she paused before going on "...thanks."

He cleared his throat. "Well, whether you want to be or not," he said, his voice gruffer than he'd planned, "you're part of the family now."

Tears welled in her eyes and left Matt dying to escape. Before he could figure out how to make that happen gracefully, Penny pulled him into a hug that caused the sword at his hip to jab him in the abdomen. Two of the longest seconds of his life later, Penny pulled back and reached on tiptoe to plant a kiss on Matt's cheek.

Which was nicer than he'd thought it would be, but all he really wanted was to find Callie and grab a few minutes alone. Penny shot him a beautiful smile, spun on her heel and took off.

Feeling a little lighter, he watched his soon-to-be sister-in-law thread her way through the crowd. At least the weekend weather appeared to be behaving for tomorrow's wedding. The sunny days came complete with a cool breeze and mild temperatures. Good thing, too, seeing how most of the guests were dressed for the times. No shorts or tank tops or T-shirts, just tunics and cloaks and surcoats, not to mention petticoats and peasant dresses.

He scanned the sea of colors, looking for Callie, when a hand clapped him on the back.

"Can I buy the best man a beer?"

Thwarted again.

Matt turned and hiked a brow at his kid brother. Tommy swept the brown waves of hair from his face—a

nervous habit since he'd been a little kid. The sight never
failed to trigger a swell of affection in Matt's heart.

"Mead," Matt said. "Callie very specifically in-
structed me to call it mead."

"Yeah." Tommy's brown eyes crinkled at the corners. "About Callie—"

"Beer," Matt said, fighting the scowl and hoping to
put off any further questioning. Mentioning Callie's
name had been tantamount to asking for his kid brother's harassment. "I'm definitely up for a beer."

Tommy shot Matt a look that screamed, "Nice try,
sucker," clearly communicating that Tommy was on
to his big brother's deflection technique and was only
humoring him.

For now.

Matt wasn't entirely sure why he didn't want to discuss Callie with Tommy. They'd been living in each
other's pockets for so long the reluctance felt strange.
But something about his time in New Orleans felt too
personal to discuss. A private time Matt didn't want to
share with anyone.

Including his brother.

Regardless, a small knot of tension curled low in
Matt's gut as they weaved their way through the crowd
of people, passing the strolling minstrels on their way to
the largest tent set in the middle of the field. A meeting
place, of sorts, with a crowd clearly intent on reliving
the feel of a medieval tavern.

Tommy found two empty stools at the end of a
crudely constructed wooden table. A barmaid arrived
to take their order and, as soon as she returned with
two mugs of beer, the two of them were left alone with

nothing but the noise around them and several years' worth of unresolved issues between them.

Sticking with the matter at hand seemed best.

"To you and Penny," Matt said, lifting his mug.

Tommy grinned and toasted Matt back. When his brother took a drink and set his beer down, the determined look on his face left Matt wishing he could go back to throwing another ax, even if it meant risking getting booed by a large crowd.

"There's something I've wanted to ask you," Tommy said.

Matt felt like a fool for not meeting his brother's eyes. "Fire away."

"What's up with you and Callie?"

Matt lifted his gaze to his brother's brown eyes—puppy eyes, their mother had called them. Funny how Matt had forgotten about that until just now. But she'd been right. Tommy had the same look that managed to look happy and sad, wise and innocent, all at the same time.

Matt shrugged. "We've decided not to label the relationship just yet."

Long-distance was the only label that fit. But the idea totally sucked. He'd been down the long-distance relationship road before. He couldn't imagine this time would end any prettier.

"But you're sleeping with her," Tommy said.

Frowning, Matt ran his thumb up his mug, staring at the trail left behind in the condensation. Not being the kind to kiss and tell left him in a bit of a quandary. He only had two choices, to either share too much or lie. And neither sat right with Matt.

Tommy let out a laugh. "Never mind. Your silence is good enough. Actually, I'm kind of relieved."

"Really?" Sleeping with Callie certainly made Matt feel better. But why the heck would Matt's relationship make *Tommy* feel better? "Why?"

A grin crept up his kid brother's face. "Because all that time you were down here in New Orleans, arranging this shindig, I felt bad that you had to be the one working out how to pull this weekend off. When a few days turned into almost two weeks…" Tommy ruffled his shaggy brown hair. "I don't have to tell you I was feeling pretty guilty."

"No worries, sport." Matt reached across the table and gave Tommy's shoulder a cuff. "You just owe me your undying allegiance for the rest of your life. Simple enough."

Matt's attempt at dodging a heavier discussion with a lighthearted response didn't work. Tommy's expression remained fixed on Matt and serious. And the look never went well for Matt.

"But before you stand up beside me tomorrow," Tommy said. "I want to say it again." Tommy leaned his elbows on the table. "I'm sorry for everything I put you through."

More than just the words, the expression on his little brother's face left Matt on edge.

Matt didn't look away, and every ounce of tease in his tone disappeared. "I know you are."

"But I also need to know that you forgive me," Tommy said.

Well, hell.

Matt sat back and stared out at the chaos beyond the tent. Forgiveness, he'd found, had been harder and harder to come by. The first relapse had been easy. The second, not so much. By the third round of rehab, for-giveness had been a huge struggle. A battle Matt had sometimes thought he wouldn't win.

But here they sat, two years later...

You can't make them keep paying for the same mis-takes over and over again.

Callie was right. Even if they had been in this very spot before, and Tommy had screwed up again. And clearly Tommy needed a truthful answer and not a glib response. Maybe Tommy had put his brother through an emotional wringer, but his hard work this past twenty-four months meant he deserved nothing less than an honest answer.

That and the fact the man was set to get married to-morrow.

Matt delivered the words while staring at his mug. "I'm not gonna lie, Tommy. It hasn't been easy." He lifted his gaze to his brother. "But...come on." Matt leaned forward and folded his arms on the table. "Why would I help arrange this weekend if I still had even a trace of resentment left? All I want is for you to be happy. I mean, look around you." He gestured toward the scene that included knights, and maidens, and trolls. Matt let out a huff of humor as he looked at his kid brother. "You think I'd go to all this trouble otherwise?"

Sam's serious face didn't budge. "Yeah, you would. You *totally* would." Despite the words, a grin slowly spread across Tommy's face, bringing the same the re-sponse from Matt. "But it's good to know that's not the case."

Matt blew out a breath, and the tension in his shoul-ders eased. "Well, now that we have all that cleared—"

"I'm not done, Matt. I need you to lighten up a little."

"Lighten up?"

"You know what I'm talking about," Tommy said.

The noise of the tent filled the air between them, and tension curled in Matt's gut. He watched a juggler wander by, wishing he could avoid the upcoming conversation.

"Look," Tommy said, "I'm getting through this, day by day. Both Penny and I. And yeah, sure—" Tommy pushed his hair back from his face "—some days it takes all I have to make it through. But I'm clean." He stared at Matt. "I'm *clean*."

Matt blinked back the pain, hating the words that needed to be said, even after all this time. He'd spent ten years watching Tommy, struggling to help him fight this demon that had him firmly in its grip. He'd never said the words before, because the sentiment had felt like a betrayal. But they needed to be said now.

I'm clean.

Because how many times had Matt heard those words?

Matt's words came out rough. "Yeah, I know you are, Tommy," he said. Two sharp heartbeats thumped by. "But for how long?"

Tommy barely registered a flinch on his face.

Jesus, Matt. You're such a bastard.

"You have to stop hovering, Matt," Tommy said. "I'm not a kid anymore."

"I know you're not."

Tommy went on as if Matt hadn't spoken. "Because you and I know there is no end point here. I'll always be at risk. Some days are so damn hard I want to curl up in a corner and cry." Tommy leaned closer, and Matt's chest ached so hard he thought his ribs would fracture. "I know you have this intense need to fix things. I know you see a problem and your first extinct is to swoop in, tough love and all. But you *can't* fix this for me. This is something I have to do all by myself."

"Maybe so." Matt set his mug on the wooden table with a *thump.* "But I can damn sure be around if you start to slip again."

Be around, stuck in a job where the typical day left Matt wishing he watched paint dry for a living. What was the point of this conversation? What could it possibly solve? Matt had been examining Tommy's problem from every possible angle for the past ten years. And as far as he figured, there was only one solution.

"Now if were done with the best man talk," Matt said, easing his words with a gentle pat on Tommy's back. "I've got another ax-throwing competition to lose."

CHAPTER NINE

OVER THE PAST ten years, Callie had sometimes wondered if she'd been fooling herself about her life. Today Callie had determined with absolutely certainty that her mistake all those years ago had been both the worst and the best turning point of her life.

If she hadn't blown that scholarship she'd probably be working for someone else right now, because that would have been the safer, easier route to take. But when her choices had been limited to only one—that one choice being whatever she could build herself from the ground up—she'd set about and done just that.

With the most important event in the history of Callie's business currently taking place right before her eyes.

The day of the Paulson-Smith wedding began just as beautifully as the day before. The grassy field was dotted with white tents that flapped in the cool breeze, providing a sharp contrast against the crystal-blue sky. A crowd of guests dressed in their best medieval fair, maidens and princesses and knights stood next to wizards and trolls. Penny's silver silk gown shimmered around her slender figure and made her look like an elegant elf.

Gorgeous.

The crowd had grown from online gaming friends to several hundred interested well-wishers. From the three news cameras mixed in with the crowd, clearly the publicity would be bigger than even Colin had guessed. With her ex, along with Penny and Tommy, set to be interviewed during the reception, the day clearly promised to be a boon for Callie's business.

So how come all she could focus on was Matt?

With about eight other things she should be checking on, Callie shaded her eyes from the sun, grinning as a chain-mail-wearing Matt walked Penny down a makeshift aisle composed of friends dressed as knights, swords drawn and creating an arch over a red carpet leading to the front of a gorgeous canopy. The sight created a happy thrum in Callie's veins. Publicity aside, the scene was the single most satisfying event in her life to date.

But Matt wearing chain mail would never cease to be Callie's favorite part. And while he protested that he was no one's knight in shining armor, she begged to differ. The smile on the bride's face, and the almost embarrassed look on Matt's, brought about a pressure in Callie's chest.

An emotion she couldn't name.

Feeling like a sappy fool, Callie grinned as she discreetly wiped the tears gathering at the corners of her eyes. Tommy looked happy. Penny positively beamed. And Matt, the man who played the largest role in ensuring this ceremony happened, looked adorably embarrassed and charmingly put out. He'd stuck by his brother and refused to give up when things got tough. And, no matter how silly Matt thought the whole affair, he'd thrown himself into making sure today took place just how Tommy and Penny wanted.

A buzzing started in her chest, creating a warmth that had nothing to do with the sun or the crowd pressing in around her.

Standing on the other side of the makeshift aisle, Colin discreetly waved at Callie and then pointed at his watch. They'd caught up earlier and planned on running through the best way to handle the news interviews set to take place after the ceremony. Which she was about twenty minutes late for.

She knew she should slip away and meet up as planned, but she couldn't force her feet to move. Callie blinked and glanced back up the aisle, unable to shift her gaze from Matt as he leaned in for Penny's kiss. Or when he stepped forward to stand by Tommy.

The buzzing grew stronger. Callie pressed her hand to her chest as the pressure became a physical ache, the realization washing over her with all the gentleness of a tidal wave.

She loved him.

The terrifying and wonderful and life-altering realization kept her rooted in place. Even as Colin managed to unobtrusively weave his way through the crowd of people craning to watch the small three-person bridal party make their way beneath the white awning covering the wooden platform—a last-minute addition ensuring the larger than expected crowd could see the ceremony.

But all Callie wanted to watch was Matt, in his chain mail and leggings and boots and the sword hanging at his side. A small grin on his face as he watched Tommy take Penny's hand and step in front of the officiant dressed as, of all things, a wizard.

And falling for the man who lived a thousand miles away felt significantly more terrifying than failing at this publicity event.

Jeez, what had she done?

A hand lightly gripped her elbow, but she didn't budge as Colin whispered in her ear.

"We were supposed to meet twenty minutes ago," he said.

"I know."

Still, she didn't move. No matter how many times she told her feet to start walking.

"What's the matter?" Colin leaned forward, his gaze landing on her face. "Good God, Callie. What's gotten into you?"

She stared up at Colin, her mind still stuck on her personal epiphany. And then she felt a drop of water hit her cheek. Concerned, Callie glanced up at the sky. Still no clouds. She touched her face and finally realized she was still crying.

Despite her ridiculously romantic ideals, she'd never cried at a wedding before. Of course, realizing she'd fallen hard for the brother of the groom was a first, too.

Concern clouded Colin's voice. "Are you okay?"

Callie didn't respond, simply watched Tommy and Penny begin to repeat their vows. And the signal that the ceremony was quickly coming to a close provided the impetus to move. With one last lingering look at Matt on stage, hands clasped behind his back, eyes fixed on his little brother, Callie turned and followed Colin silently through the throng of people to a quiet spot well away from the crowd and the ceremony.

Colin still looked at her as if she were about to go off the deep end. "Callie, are you sick?"

"No." She shook her head, hoping the motion would clear her spinning brain.

No such luck.

Colin crossed his arms, a skeptical look creeping up his face. "I know you love weddings. But this is kind of over the top, even for you."

She wiped her cheek again and found her cheek just as wet as before. Good grief, she felt as if she'd sprung a leak.

"So what's wrong?" Colin asked.

She stared up at her ex, a million responses flitting through her brain before the only one that fit came out.

"I love him."

Colin suddenly looked as though he'd prefer to be identified as the evil Zhorg and taken into custody by the crowd to be hanged by the neck until dead. And then drawn and quartered. Followed by a massive festival as the townsfolk danced while he burned, his body cremated just to be sure the deed was done.

Her ex's eyes shifted from Callie's face to the focus of her gaze, the small party standing on stage, and then back to Callie again.

Worry laced his tone. "I hope you're talking about Matt and not Tommy."

Forcing back the bubble of hysterical laughter, mostly triggered by panic, Callie rolled her eyes. "Of course I'm talking about Matt."

"Good." Colin winced. "Because falling for a man who just walked down the aisle probably wouldn't end well."

A surge of fear hit. "Matt lives in Manford, Michigan. A thousand miles away."

"I'm sure y'all can work something out."

She wished she felt so optimistic. And why hadn't she concerned herself with this detail before? Suddenly pulling off a fabulous event without losing her focus seemed a terribly stupid reason for avoiding a relationship with Matt. But this? Falling in love with a man who lived so far away? One who clearly felt responsible for his brother?

She'd only just begun to realize how complicated their relationship was.

Callie had ten years—and most of her identity—invested in Fantasy Weddings. Her business wasn't portable. She couldn't just pick up and start over again. And she loved New Orleans. Her family was here. Her friends were here.

The tension in Callie's stomach expanded.

"Hey." Colin laid his hand on Callie's shoulder. "Now's not the time to fall apart, okay?"

The concern in his face only highlighted how truly screwed she was. She wiped her cheeks and forced herself back to the matter at hand. "Of course not. I can handle this." She tried for a confidence-inspiring smile, hoping it didn't feel as weak as it felt. "Let's go talk to the news crew and figure out the best place for the interviews."

Right.

Interviews.

Medieval wedding reception.

Dungeons of Zhorg.

Callie turned her back on the end of the ceremony—and the view of Matt standing on stage—and followed

Colin in the direction of the news crews. Focusing on getting through the rest of the day appeared to be her only option.

The sun was setting as Callie forced herself to focus on the staff taking down the tents. When Matt came up beside her, she gave strict instructions to her heart to calm down. Much to her distress, her instructions went ignored when he slipped an arm around her waist.

"You okay?" he asked.

"Absolutely."

Her smile felt forced, and Callie knew Matt suspected something, but she concentrated on remaining calm so she could finish her job. During the reception, Tommy and Penny's brief interview had come out really cute, mostly because they were both so ridiculously happy. Callie had no doubt their two minutes of fame would be well received by viewers. As the maker of the video game, Colin's interview was less emotional. But Colin was more than just a geeky gamer. He excelled as the marketing guru, as well. His smooth, well-polished blurb mentioning Fantasy Weddings and the *Dungeons of Zhorg* sounded casual and didn't come across rehearsed at all.

"How much longer before I can get you alone again?" Matt murmured, a crooked smile on his face.

She discreetly fished her small pocket watch from the bodice of her princess dress, her favorite costume to date. The overdress of robin's-egg-blue split in front, forming an inverted V to showcase the design of the white satin and gold brocade pattern beneath.

And, despite the fear now curled around her spine

and setting up house, she had to laugh at the expression on Matt's face.

"I was thinking I'd like to get you out of that dress and see how you'd look in chain mail." His sex-filled smile started a thrumming vibration in her belly and spread outward. "With nothing underneath. So…" he said.

He leaned in close, sending a spike in her pulse, heat between her legs and anxiety twisting in her stomach.

"How long?" he finished.

"My assistant volunteered to oversee the cleanup," she said. "And I already spoke to the vendor who supplied the table and chairs, so I'm free to go."

Free to go.

Free to go where? Back to her place with Matt and have sex? Or free to go back to her regularly scheduled life, the one without Matt in it?

"Perfect," Matt said, steering her in the direction of the parking lot.

Swallowing hard, she glanced down at her dress and smoothed a hand down her skirt. "How did your week at Manford Memorial go?"

"As uneventful as ever," Matt replied.

She pounced on the one thing she knew for sure. Matt held no deep abiding affection for his job or his hometown. Surely that meant he'd be willing to move? No matter how much she loved him, she simply couldn't afford to start all over again.

Desperate for something to do with her hands beside reach for Matt, she picked up her skirt as she walked. "Have you ever thought about living somewhere other than Manford?"

Matt shot her a guarded look, the expression doing

little to ease her nerves. So she hurried on before she lost her courage completely.

"You know, find a new job?" she said.

"Why should I?" His steps slowed a little, making it easier to match his stride. But his tone was wary. "It's home."

Her feet fumbled, and Matt reached out briefly to steady her. Jeez, his hand on her arm wasn't helping to calm her down. But she couldn't just take him home to her bed without finding out more.

Callie opened her mouth to speak but failed at making a sound. She swallowed hard, forcing her mouth to cooperate. "But have you ever considered taking a part-time job somewhere else?" She glanced at him out of the corner of her eye. "Moving your home base?"

Matt kept his eyes firmly ahead. "Like where?"

The loaded question felt like a shotgun aimed at her heart. Was he avoiding her gaze because he wasn't sure of the direction of the conversation? Or did he know and simply wanted to avoid the topic altogether? One thing she knew for sure, she'd never know unless she asked. And sleeping with Matt now that she'd figured out she loved him would make letting him go harder in the end.

"Like here," she said. "In New Orleans."

Several seconds passed with only the sound of the gravel beneath their shoes, and Callie felt every crunch like a kick to the chest.

"I could certainly look into doing recurrent shifts as a traveling doc in their E.R.," he said.

Not exactly the answer she wanted to hear. But the response felt encouraging.

"How often could you get down this way?" she asked.

"I could pull off six, maybe seven days a month."

Six days a month? And he'd be working busy shifts. What kind of life would that be for the two of them?

Callie came to a stop and stared up at him. "That's not much time."

A small breeze kicked up, and the setting sun finally sank beneath the tops of the oak trees, casting a shadow across them both.

"Callie." With a sigh, Matt turned to face her, and she could see the conflict in his expression. "I can't leave Manford."

The words sliced through her like a sharp blade through whipped cream cheese.

"Why not?" she asked.

Matt looked out across the parking lot. Several seconds ticked by. Callie expected him to come up with something noteworthy, given the amount of time he spent formulating his response. But when the words came they were incredibly disappointing in their simplicity.

"It's my home," he said.

Callie slowly inhaled, searching for strength, before blowing out her breath in one long exhale.

"People move all the time, Matt," she said. "And it's not as if you love your job there." She waited for him to look at her again. When he kept his eyes on the park, the trees fading as dusk claimed the rest of the landscape, she went on, "I know you don't. So don't even try to pretend that you do."

"I never said I did."

She stepped closer. "So move down here." Callie longed to get some sort of a response from the man. When nothing was forthcoming, she tried again. "Make

New Orleans your home base. Tommy's married now, Matt. He's moving on with his life."

Callie died a million deaths waiting for him to respond.

"I know," he said.

Did he? Tommy seemed to be moving on with his life. But not Matt.

"Are you planning on going on the honeymoon with them?" she asked dryly.

"Jesus, of course not."

Fear and frustration made her words harder than she'd intended. "Then why not move?"

Matt strode several feet away before stopping, his back to her. He shoved his hands into his hair, leaving sandy tufts sticking up. When he finally turned to face her again, the look on his face was one she'd never seen before.

"The last time I left Tommy for too long I came home and found him unconscious on the couch." He stared off in the distance, and she knew by the look on his face he was seeing now what he'd seen back then. "He'd gone through rehab number four and had been doing well for months. But I knew right away he wasn't just sleeping. Everything was off. The room felt wrong. Tommy looked wrong. Damn, the very air in the room felt wrong. I couldn't wake up him up. And—"

His voice grew so hoarse it died out, and Callie reached out to gently wrap her fingers around his wrist, the look on his face heartbreaking.

"For two seconds I couldn't find a pulse," he said.

A chill swept up her spine and traveled out her limbs. Goose bumps pricked her arms, the hair at the back of her neck standing on end. Matt's words came out rushed.

"And suddenly all the tough love you've come to accept as necessary just doesn't matter anymore," he said.

"He's been clean for two years, Matt," she said softly.

"Which is why I started taking the occasional locums jobs in Miami and Los Angeles. But I can't be gone that long."

"I'm in love with you."

The stunned look on Matt's face would have been funny if she hadn't been hurting so much. She hadn't meant to say the words yet. And she certainly hadn't meant for them to come out the way they did. So plain. With no lead-in. Nothing, no sign from her to prepare Matt for what would follow. But maybe the simple statement would knock some sense into the man.

Callie stared at Matt, her mind spinning as she tried to make sense of the words. At first she thought his resistance simply meant he didn't feel as much for her as she felt for him. But the look on Matt's face now told her the truth. He did care about her. No telling how much, but enough that he clearly didn't want to leave. But he just couldn't let his worries about Tommy go.

Matt had suffered so much through the years, and his fear for Tommy was deeply entrenched. There'd be no reaching the man with easy words. She was going to have to be brutally, brutally honest with him to get him to see reason. He loved his brother too much, had suffered too much to let the issue go easily.

And, as hard as it was going to be, she had to fight. She deserved a chance at happiness. And Matt deserved so much more than he had in his current life.

She steeled herself against the pain she knew was sure to follow. "So that's what this is about."

Matt's expression grew guarded. When he said nothing, she went on, no matter how much it hurt him in turn. Matt couldn't be allowed to continue to sacrifice himself, not when her bluntly harsh words had a chance of getting him to see how much more he deserved out of life. "What is with you and this martyr complex?" she said.

"I don't know what you're talking about."

"Yes, you do," she said softly.

"Look, is this really necessary? I'd hoped to enjoy the rest of my time in New Orleans with you."

Anger flared, pushing the tender feelings to the back of the line. "And that will be...what? Two, maybe three days?" She forced herself to maintain his gaze. Heart thumping, she tried to keep the bitterness at bay, but his unwillingness to even consider a change hurt like hell. "I understand you want to stick around and be there for Tommy if he needs you. And I suppose you have to do what you think is right. But I can't do this anymore."

"Do what?"

"Love you. Settle for a few days here and there. I've put my life on hold and now that I've rediscovered how much life there is to live outside of work, I don't want to settle anymore."

Matt stared off into the shadows growing along the trees lining the park. A muscle in his jaw ticked, and, for the second time that day, Callie fought the tears of frustration and anger and pain that were gathering at the corners of her lids. He didn't look torn, signaling she at least had some room to convince him to change his mind. He looked resigned.

And that hurt worst of all.

"You're right," he said. "You shouldn't have to settle for whatever time I get to snatch here and there. You deserve a full-time relationship, not a part-time one. You also deserve better than to continue to endure your mother's insinuation that you've settled for less with your job. Maybe you should tell her exactly how you feel instead of letting your guilt keep you silent."

Matt unlocked her car and opened the door for her. Muscles tight, head aching, heart hurting, she gathered up her dress and slid into the driver's seat, fabric billowing around her legs. She gripped the steering wheel and willed herself to calm the heck down so she could at least say goodbye without sounding like a total wreck.

Hand on the roof her car, Matt leaned in to press his lips to hers.

"Goodbye, Callie. Thanks for making Tommy and Penny's day special."

Matt straightened up and stared down at her for three more heartbeats. And then he turned and headed across the parking lot.

CHAPTER TEN

ONE WEEK LATER, Callie sat in her office and twisted off the top of her bottled water, staring at her laptop in the center of her desk. As she tried to compose a reasonable answer to her latest *Ex Factor* question, she avoided looking at the tiny camera eye centered at the top of the computer screen. And desperately tried not to remember how Matt had looked the night of their Skype sex.

She pressed her palms over her eyes. Maybe if she pushed hard enough she could force the images from her brain. Unfortunately, her brain was still filled with visions of Matt wearing nothing, long muscular legs stretched out before him. The broad shoulders and the hard chest and the flat abdomen. She loved the way his sweatpants had been slung low over his lean hips. Better still? Those sexy hands satisfying his body while she urged him on with her words. The sight of the successful conclusion would be her undoing for some time to come.

Throat dry as yesterday's leftover toast, she reached for her bottle of water and swallowed gratefully.

She might never be able to sit through a video conference again without thinking of that moment. A fact that would prove incredibly inconvenient today when she'd had a Skype session with the mother of the bride of next week's *Pride and Prejudice* wedding.

But of all the things she missed about Matt, many a sexy episode aside, she missed his smile the most. The sexy half smirk, that teasing hint of a grin. And her favorite? The smile accompanied by that spark of full-on humor in his eyes. She wished she could hang a poster on her wall with all the various looks. But that would only remind her of what was missing in her life.

And that something was Matt.

Callie slumped in her seat. The first few days after the wedding, she'd hoped that he'd call her up to say he'd rethought his position. But as one day slipped into the next, she began to wonder if she should consider moving. But leaving New Orleans, her family and her business?

She couldn't imagine life so far away from the city, the bayou of her childhood and Aunt Billie. As strained as their relationship was, she'd even miss her parents. And she'd just started reconnecting with the extended family she hadn't seen in years. She couldn't leave now.

A knock sounded on her door and a head full of brown hair poked through.

Callie sat up in surprise. "Mama."

Her mother rarely came to visit at the office. Usually it was Callie making the trip across town to see her parents.

"Hi, honey. You look...off," her mom said.

A sad smile crept up Callie's face. "I'm feeling very off."

Her mother settled into the seat across from Callie and folded her arms across her lap. She looked ready to wait until Callie explained.

"The Paulson wedding was a huge success," Callie said

"So I heard. That's nice."

Nice.

Snippets of the event had been broadcast on two local cable channels. Tommy and Penny's brief interview had been picked up by a syndicated news channel and been aired across the country. Callie had received more business inquires in the past week than ever before. Business was booming, and Callie would probably need to hire extra help to keep up with the work.

But all she got from her mother was *nice*.

"What happened with that doctor you brought to the reunion?" her mother said.

The muscles in Callie's stomach clinched. Something in her mother's voice rubbed Callie wrong. It was the same tone she'd used the first time they discussed Callie's screwup in college. The tone that held an implied "What now?" Ten years later and her mother still expected bad news at every turn. And, as bad news went, this was the worst Callie had ever experienced.

Matt…*gone.*

And if she could blurt out the truth to Matt, there seemed no point in keeping anything from her mother now. "I'm in love with Matt Paulson."

Something flickered in her mother's eyes, but her expression didn't budge. "I figured out as much on my own."

"You did?"

"Well, I am your mother." Her mother shrugged, as if the act of giving birth to Callie somehow had provided Belle LaBeau a peephole into Callie's heart. "And it's not like you did a very good job of hiding the fact. I could tell by the way you looked at him at the reunion. When he laughed, your whole face would light up." She hesitated and then smoothed a hand down her pants. "You certainly never looked at Colin like that."

This time Callie did groan. Good God. How long before her mother let this issue go? Callie had recovered from the breakup years ago. Did her mother need therapy to get past this and move on?

"Mama, Colin and I have been over for years. He's happily married to a woman I consider a friend."

"I'm well aware of that." A soft smile appeared on her mother's face. "I happen to know the woman who planned the wedding."

In the end, Callie lost her battle with a wry grin.

"I'm not stuck on Colin," her mother went on.

The news surprised Callie, because she sure couldn't tell by her mother's action. Every single visit with her mom had ended with Colin being mentioned at some point in time.

Callie sat up straighter in her seat. "Then why are you constantly bringing him up?"

"Only because he's the last man you've brought around to visit your family. At least, he was until Matt came along."

The mention of Matt's name brought a fresh wave of pain, her heart aching. Callie shifted her focus to the window that overlooked the warehouse district of New Orleans. The day sunny and bright, but inside Callie's office felt dark.

"You're happy arranging weddings for other people, yet you haven't had a serious relationship in ages," her mother said. "What happened with Matt?"

Callie's voice sounded as hollow as she felt. "He went

back home to Michigan. And he's kind of stuck living in Manford. It's…" Callie paused trying to think of an explanation that wouldn't be an invasion of Matt's and Tommy's privacy. "It's complicated."

Her mother crossed her legs and studied Callie for a moment. And in one of those moments known horribly well by kids the world over, Callie knew her mother was about to offer advice. Whether Callie wanted it or not.

"You could move up to Michigan," she said. "Maybe even finally realize your dream of finishing college."

Callie's heart slowly slipped to her toes.

"I don't want to go back to college," Callie said.

"But that was all you talked about in high school."

"That was the dream of an eighteen-year-old who had no real idea what she wanted to do with her life," Callie said. "It was always more your dream than mine."

Her mother looked knocked flat, and a stab of guilt struck Callie again. She never meant to be quite so truthful.

"Look, Mama," Callie said. "I'm sorry you and Dad sacrificed so much to get me into a great school."

Her mother straightened her shoulders. "Your dad and I sacrificed so you could make something of yourself."

Callie dropped her head into her hands. "Mama." Callie managed not to let out a moan. Barely. She looked up again. "I love my job." She dropped her hands to her desk and met the brown gaze of her mother sitting on the other side. "This is exactly where I want to be. I'm my own boss and I have a very successful business. I appreciate all you and Dad have done for me, but—"

It was past time she told the truth and stopped letting this issue slide. She couldn't continue to remain silent.

Callie sucked in a breath and gathered her courage. "But I'm not sorry about how things turned out. I wouldn't change anything even if I *could*. If I could climb into a time capsule and undo all I'd done in college, I wouldn't." She should have spoken these words ages ago. Callie steadily held her mother's gaze. "I'm exactly where I want to be," Callie said, "doing exactly what I want to do."

The strength of the conviction in her words reminded her exactly why she couldn't drop her life and move up to Michigan. Both her mother's brows arched in surprise, and Callie let the words settle a little deeper before going on.

"This isn't my second-choice life, Mama. This is my very *best* life."

Or at least it had been until she lost Matt.

Callie pushed the crushing thought aside and concentrated on meeting her mother's gaze. "And I need—"

When Callie's voice gave out, her mother set her purse on the floor beside her chair. "What do you need?"

"I need to stop feeling like y'all are just waiting for me to screw up again."

Silence filled the room and Callie did her best not to shift her gaze away from her mother. It felt as if Callie had lived and died a thousand lives as she waited for her mother to speak.

"Okay," her mother said.

Callie blinked. *Okay?* Just like that?

"Now you need to do me a favor, Callie."

Callie fought to keep her breathing steady. "What's that?"

Her mother leaned forward, her eyes intent. "Stop

avoiding relationships. Get serious about finding someone, about sharing your *future,* with someone."

Callie's lungs stopped functioning, and she longed to
take a deep breath. Problem was, she had finally gone
out and gotten serious about someone.

But he was gone for good.

"Why are you still here?"

Tommy's voice echoed off the walls of the garage,
and Matt turned from his task of sorting through his
tools. "Excuse me?"

Matt had been banging around the garage for the past
two hours, trying to pack for the move to an apartment
that held little appeal, yet grateful for the mindless task
of sorting through his stuff. He'd tossed the things he
didn't need—a pile that wasn't as big as it should have
been—and stacked the stuff yet to be packed, which
was larger than need be. Boxes covered the floor of his
bedroom and living room and perched on the counters
in the kitchen. He couldn't seem to decide what to keep
and what to throw away. So two hours ago Matt had
come out to the garage, frustrated by his inability to
focus, thinking that dividing the supply of tools in half
would be an easier process.

He'd never had trouble focusing before. If anything,
his focus had always been a problem. But with his mind
stuck on missing Callie, and the impossible situation a
relationship with her presented, he'd come out to sort
through his problem the only way he knew how: banging the wrenches and screwdrivers and the various-
size hammers around. The process offered him some
satisfaction.

But zero relief.

"You heard me," his brother said.

Tommy stepped down into the garage. His wavy brown hair and brown eyes always made him look a bit like an overgrown puppy. Well, an overgrown puppy with serious issues.

His brother came to a halt beside Matt and leaned his hip against the workbench.

"How long are we going to tiptoe around this, Matt?"

Silence had been working for them so far. And Matt wasn't sure he knew how to change the status quo.

"I don't know what you're talking about," Matt said.

But he did. The dark thoughts plaguing him since he'd left New Orleans had been following him around like a black cloud hell-bent on raining down on his head, complete with lightning bolts and thunder and the foul mood.

Tommy let out a scoff. "You don't want to be here." He waved his hand to encompass their current surroundings, but Matt knew he was referencing something much bigger than a garage located in Manford, Michigan. "You want to be in New Orleans." Brown eyes gazed at Matt. "With *Callie*."

The familiar ache in his chest friggin' hurt.

"Maybe," Matt said.

Yes, his mind screamed.

Matt turned away from his brother and concentrated on repacking the tools in a manner worthy of the most diehard of obsessive compulsives. Matt knew the statistics; crystal meth addicts had one of the highest relapse rates of all the drug users.

There was no answer to this one.

Just like Tommy's addiction, this wasn't a problem Matt could fix. There was no treatment to be applied that cured the disease. Frustration burned through Matt and he randomly picked up a wrench and rubbed his finger on the cool metal.

"But my home is here," Matt said.

"It doesn't have to be."

Matt closed his eyes, his fingers curling around a Phillips head screwdriver.

"Manford doesn't have to be your home base any-more," Tommy went on. "In fact, you could take a per-manent job in New Orleans. The emergency rooms there have to be busy enough to satisfy the adrenaline junky in you."

"I could," Matt said. "But I won't."

"Why not?"

Matt stared out the window at the bleak view that only appeared that way because he was in freaking *Manford*. Anxiety coiled in his stomach, and he decided to voice the words that had been bouncing around his head for years.

"Because when I walked in on you two years ago, for several seconds I thought you were dead."

The ache in his chest was all-consuming, and he met his brother's brown eyes again. They'd never discussed that day. The event had been too painful. Matt took in the way Tommy's hair flopped on his forehead, just like it had as a kid.

"And I can't bear to go through that again," Matt said.

"So what does that mean?" Tommy cocked his head. "Tough love until the day I die?"

Matt's lips twisted. "*Tough* is a pretty good word for it," he said. But as the moment lingered between them, Matt finally went on, "No matter what, you're my brother. That comes before everything else."

Tommy cleared his throat as his eyes grew suspiciously bright. "I told you before, you can't save me from myself, Matt," he said softly. And then he let out a humorless huff. "Though God knows you've tried." He rolled his head, as if releasing the tension in his neck. "You can't put your entire life on hold anymore," Tommy continued. "You have to let it go, Matt."

Anger, bright and hot, surged from his core. "What the hell?" Matt braced himself as he faced Tommy. "You're my brother, Tommy. How am I supposed to just let you go?"

"Not me," Tommy said. "The guilt."

The word slammed into Matt, leaving him gut-punched and short of breath. His ribs squeezing his heart so hard Matt was sure the pressure would crush him.

What is with you and this martyr complex?

Jesus, he'd told Callie to fully let go of the past, and here he was clinging to his. But Tommy didn't know about the thoughts he'd had...

Matt let out a self-deprecating scoff, wishing Callie was here with him with that playful spark in her eyes and her honey-tinted drawl. And the kind of nonjudgmental understanding that let a person share even the worst truths about themselves without fear.

Because how could he share that brutal news with his kid brother? He opted for the easier explanation instead.

Matt left the tool bench and headed for the stairs leading to the kitchen, dropping down to sit on the bottom step. "I should have been around more in the beginning."

"You had a medical degree you were trying to earn." Tommy took a seat beside Matt.

"But Mom and Dad were gone, and we were alone."

And God knows wading through the days, trying to figure out how to deal with Tommy and be an adult all at the same time hadn't been easy.

They sat there, side by side, and Matt tried to push the memories of the first time he'd found Tommy passed out on the floor. Of a Tommy so gaunt, so thin, his color so unhealthy that it physically hurt to look at him. Sure, Matt had been checking in by phone. But only so much information can be gleaned from the sound of a voice.

He couldn't remember the precise moment he began to have his suspicions something was off. The little niggles of doubt had always been easily rationalized away.

He's having an off week.

He's stressed.

He's just not hungry today.

Of getting the call he'd wrecked his car again, and this time not being sure Tommy was going to pull through. Perhaps the time had come to explain to Tommy exactly how much Matt didn't deserve his kid brother's devotion.

Matt stared straight ahead. He couldn't meet Tommy's eyes, not with what he was about to say.

"The third time you walked out of rehab and waded back into that mess it took everything in me not to leave." Matt closed his eyes as he remembered the turbulent thoughts from that day. Angry. Petrified. And knowing he just couldn't live this life anymore.

Tommy remained quiet beside him while silence engulfed the garage. Matt couldn't bring himself to look at his brother. The confession was hard enough to express without those wide, brown eyes staring at him. He felt like crap for sharing the thoughts with his brother. If they'd just been a fleeting thought Matt wouldn't feel so guilty. But since that day, every morning he'd woken up with the same thought.

Leave.

Get out of town.

Save yourself.

He scrubbed his face with his hands, exhausted from the mental war being waged in his head. And so friggin' sick of living his life in limbo he didn't know what to do. With every one of those thoughts came the opposing thought. Tommy was all the family Matt had. Walking away felt impossible, even during those times Matt was sure he was drowning.

"God, you have no idea just how badly I wanted to pack up and get the hell out of Dodge. Go to the farthest city that I could." He turned to meet his brother's gaze. "Because I just couldn't bear the torture of waiting around for you to finally kill yourself. Watching you waste away into someone I didn't recognize anymore."

Always braced for the next slip. The next call from the E.R. The next night Tommy didn't come home and Matt was sure that he'd overdosed, unconscious.

Or dead.

"I just couldn't stand to have my heart broken again," Matt said.

Tommy's voice sounded raw. "But you didn't go."

Matt's lips twisted at the words. They might as well be inscribed on his tombstone.

"But it's time," Tommy said. "You've got to get on with your life and stop worrying about your kid brother. Go back to Callie, Matt." Tommy's brown gaze held

Matt's hostage, and then his brother grinned. "Before you become a grumpy old man no one wants to be around anymore. Cuz, you know, you're already half-way there."

Matt slowly sucked in a breath. He'd told Callie to get over the guilt, maybe it was time he followed his own advice.

He let out a scoff. "Is this my kid brother giving me advice?"

"This is your kid brother showing you some tough love, dude, because it's my turn. You need to leave. I need you to leave." Tommy crossed his arms and leaned back against the railing. "How can I ever be sure I've made it on my own if you're always around to help me out? I've kicked the ugly addiction. Every day I'm concentrating on staying clean. I know you've tried to ease my way in the world by smoothing out the bumps along the way. Now it's time for me to handle life on my own."

Matt's chest shook with the force of the pounding beneath his ribs.

"Go back to New Orleans. Take a job there. You can visit whenever you like. This will always be your home, too." Tommy stood up, looking down at Matt. "But you belong with Callie."

Tommy climbed the last two steps and entered the kitchen, closing the door behind him. Matt stared at the door, his brother's parting words echoing in his brain.

CHAPTER ELEVEN

THE WALTZ STARTED, and the bride and groom headed for the center of the room, the ballroom of the River-way plantation transformed into an eighteenth-century ball. Callie watched, holding her breath as the bridal party joined in. They'd only had two days to rehearse the dance, and certainly no time to practice in their Regency-era wedding outfits.

With the bride's dark hair upswept and adorned with baby's breath, curls pinned to her head, imagining her as Elizabeth Bennet required very little stretch of the imagination. The groom, however, wasn't quite tall enough to pull off a convincing Fitzwilliam Darcy. But the man wore the cravat and waistcoat with pride.

Callie was enjoying the results of her hard work when a voice interrupted her thoughts.

"So, will there be zombies invading this reception?"

Callie whirled and came face-to-face with Matt, and the sight sent Callie's senses soaring. In a waistcoat, white linen cravat and pantaloons, he looked unusually formal yet still good enough to eat.

"Could be a fitting end, don't you think?" he finished with an easy smile.

Callie tried to reply, her mouth parting, but no words formed.

Was he here to convince her to reconsider a long-distance relationship? Or was he here to tell her he'd changed his mind and that he was ready to let his little brother go? Maybe he was finally ready to move on from a life that including the two brothers living in a constant state of protector and the protected. Callie knew the situation had been necessary during the beginnings of Tommy's recovery days—the by-product being two men who didn't know how to simply be brothers, instead of recovering addict and responsible older brother.

Callie fisted her hand behind her back, resisting the urge to grip the lapel of Matt's coat and haul him closer. She longed to ask him the questions swirling in her brain, questions like *Why are you here?* or *Have you changed your mind?*

Or more important: *Do you love me as much as I love you?*

"No," she said. "No zombies."

"That's too bad," he said.

"Depends on who you ask."

Not the conversation she'd have predicted would take place upon seeing Matt again. Not only did she not know where to start, she was almost afraid to find out the answers. If he was here to convince her to change her mind and accept less, she just might cave.

And even as her head was telling her to be strong, her heart was breaking a little more.

"Walk with me a moment?" he asked.

Pulse picking up its pace, she said, "Sure."

Callie followed Matt out the French doors and onto the veranda, trying to convince herself to stay true to her goals.

But the past few weeks had only gotten harder, not easier, and she wasn't entirely sure she had the strength to resist a part-time relationship offer again. Not when every morning started with her missing Matt, his laugh and his dry sense of humor. And every evening ending up with her staring up at the ceiling of her room, dreaming of having him back in her bed. In her life.

But all that seemed too much to ask after two weeks of no contact.

"How did you pull off the outfit?" she asked instead.

He turned and leaned against the wrought-iron railing, the branches of the oak tree beyond lit by the light from the ballroom.

"I phoned Colin and spoke with Jamie," Matt said. "Turns out your ex's wife was very eager to help me arrange a romantic meet up with you. She insisted this would be an opportune moment. Even phoned the bride and groom to ensure I'd be welcome."

A small laugh escaped Callie. "That explains the looks they were giving me at the rehearsal dinner last night."

Matt grinned. "Beware the romantic musings of those who are about to get married. Unfortunately—" he looked down at his clothes "—everyone thought it best I blend in."

"Why are you here, other than to make the most delicious Fitzwilliam Darcy ever?"

She probably shouldn't have added in the last part.

She should be playing it cool. She should be holding her feelings closer to her chest. But she couldn't.

"I came tonight hoping to make an impression," he said.

Afraid to breathe, Callie asked, "What kind of impression?"

Matt stepped closer, instantly swamping her senses. The warm breeze ruffled his sandy hair and held a hint of magnolias, but all Callie could register was Matt's scent of fresh citrusy soap. The heat from his body. The sizzle in those hazel eyes.

His eyes never left hers. "'I have been meditating on the very great pleasure which a pair of fine eyes in the face of a pretty woman can bestow.'"

Two seconds passed before the words fully registered in her brain.

Stunned, Callie reached out and gripped the sleeve of Matt's waist coat. "You read *Pride and Prejudice?*"

A slow smile crept up his face.

"How else is a man supposed to impress a woman who arranges fantasy weddings for a living?" he asked. "Quoting Darcy seemed like a good place to start."

Too afraid to hope, Callie remained silent, her grip on his sleeve growing tight.

"I just got started on the paperwork to obtain privileges at St. Matthews Hospital," Matt went on. "Turns out they have a need for a few more E.R. docs."

Heart hammering, she had to ask, "For locums work?"

"Nope," he said. "Full-time. Well, 80 percent time, anyway. Because that will leave me some room to do an occasional locums shift up in Manford."

Afraid to burst the budding hope in her heart, Callie hiked an eyebrow, and Matt smiled.

"Only one week every three months or so. That will give me plenty of time to visit my brother and his wife." His lips twitched, as if holding back a smile. "Especially now that I'm going to be an uncle."

The last was delivered so nonchalantly that several seconds passed before the news registered.

Callie let out an embarrassing whoop and launched herself into Matt's arms. He folded his arms around her, and she realized her feet were still dangling off the ground. But she didn't care. She basked in the feel of his embrace and the ever-growing realization that finally, *finally*, Matt was in New Orleans for keeps. Matt appeared in no hurry to let her down. Callie had no desire to ever let him let her go.

She buried her face in his neck and inhaled, enjoying the smell of warm skin and the feel of Matt's arms around her again. "What changed your mind?"

"Well," he said, his voice rumbling though his chest to hers. "You said you wanted me here. Tommy wanted me here. And I wanted to be here. Ultimately not being here seemed kind of stupid."

"I love your logic."

"I figured you would."

Matt set her back on her feet, but kept his arms wrapped firmly around her back, her chest pressed against his hard torso.

She looked up at him. "Did Tommy have to beat you off with a stick?"

"No." Matt's hazel eyes grew serious, and he gazed through the French doors at the couples now waltzing across the floor. "He used his own brand of tough love on me. And he agreed with your assessment. That I was good at the tough love while he was using, but I sucked after he'd quit."

"Remind me to send Tommy a huge present every year on his birthday."

"Yeah? Well, he told me he planned to send you a gift every month for getting me out of his hair. And it wasn't only logic that brought me back."

"No?"

"Yeah, there was also this little issue of me falling in love with you."

Tears gathered the corners of her eyes, and she blinked, forcing them back. How would she maintain the professional demeanor with tears in her eyes? Matt swept a strand of hair from her cheek, his fingers taking their time, and then cupped her face.

"I'm sorry it took me a while to get my head on straight," he said. "I didn't mean to make things so hard on you."

She sniffed and sent him a watery smile. "'You must learn some of my philosophy. Think only of the past as its remembrance gives you pleasure.'"

"Ah," Matt said, his lips twitching. "I love that line. And I admire Elizabeth Bennet and her practical approach to life." He eyed the front of her dress. "But I have to confess, the clothing of her era leaves a lot to be desired. Though you look beautiful, this isn't my favorite costume."

"Yeah, the A-line style doesn't exactly flatter the figure. Don't worry," she said, grinning up at Matt. "They aren't as flat as they look in this dress."

With a crooked smile, Matt leaned in and nuzzled

her neck. "No worries," he said. "I'm thinking that admiring your occasional kooky attire will keep me happily entertained for the rest of my life."

* * * * *

Mills & Boon® Hardback
June 2014

ROMANCE

MEDICAL

0514GEN STD HB

Mills & Boon® Large Print
June 2014

ROMANCE

A Bargain with the Enemy	Carole Mortimer
A Secret Until Now	Kim Lawrence
Shamed in the Sands	Sharon Kendrick
Seduction Never Lies	Sara Craven
When Falcone's World Stops Turning	Abby Green
Securing the Greek's Legacy	Julia James
An Exquisite Challenge	Jennifer Hayward
Trouble on Her Doorstep	Nina Harrington
Heiress on the Run	Sophie Pembroke
The Summer They Never Forgot	Kandy Shepherd
Daring to Trust the Boss	Susan Meier

HISTORICAL

Portrait of a Scandal	Annie Burrows
Drawn to Lord Ravenscar	Anne Herries
Lady Beneath the Veil	Sarah Mallory
To Tempt a Viking	Michelle Willingham
Mistress Masquerade	Juliet Landon

MEDICAL

From Venice with Love	Alison Roberts
Christmas with Her Ex	Fiona McArthur
After the Christmas Party...	Janice Lynn
Her Mistletoe Wish	Lucy Clark
Date with a Surgeon Prince	Meredith Webber
Once Upon a Christmas Night...	Annie Claydon

Mills & Boon® Hardback
July 2014

ROMANCE

Christakis's Rebellious Wife	Lynne Graham
At No Man's Command	Melanie Milburne
Carrying the Sheikh's Heir	Lynn Raye Harris
Bound by the Italian's Contract	Janette Kenny
Dante's Unexpected Legacy	Catherine George
A Deal with Demakis	Tara Pammi
The Ultimate Playboy	Maya Blake
Socialite's Gamble	Michelle Conder
Her Hottest Summer Yet	Ally Blake
Who's Afraid of the Big Bad Boss?	Nina Harrington
If Only...	Tanya Wright
Only the Brave Try Ballet	Stefanie London
Her Irresistible Protector	Michelle Douglas
The Maverick Millionaire	Alison Roberts
The Return of the Rebel	Jennifer Faye
The Tycoon and the Wedding Planner	Kandy Shepherd
The Accidental Daddy	Meredith Webber
Pregnant with the Soldier's Son	Amy Ruttan

MEDICAL

200 Harley Street: The Shameless Maverick	Louisa George
200 Harley Street: The Tortured Hero	Amy Andrews
A Home for the Hot-Shot Doc	Dianne Drake
A Doctor's Confession	Dianne Drake

Mills & Boon® Large Print
July 2014

ROMANCE

A Prize Beyond Jewels	Carole Mortimer
A Queen for the Taking?	Kate Hewitt
Pretender to the Throne	Maisey Yates
An Exception to His Rule	Lindsay Armstrong
The Sheikh's Last Seduction	Jennie Lucas
Enthralled by Moretti	Cathy Williams
The Woman Sent to Tame Him	Victoria Parker
The Plus-One Agreement	Charlotte Phillips
Awakened By His Touch	Nikki Logan
Road Trip with the Eligible Bachelor	Michelle Douglas
Safe in the Tycoon's Arms	Jennifer Faye

HISTORICAL

The Fall of a Saint	Christine Merrill
At the Highwayman's Pleasure	Sarah Mallory
Mishap Marriage	Helen Dickson
Secrets at Court	Blythe Gifford
The Rebel Captain's Royalist Bride	Anne Herries

MEDICAL

Her Hard to Resist Husband	Tina Beckett
The Rebel Doc Who Stole Her Heart	Susan Carlisle
From Duty to Daddy	Sue MacKay
Changed by His Son's Smile	Robin Gianna
Mr Right All Along	Jennifer Taylor
Her Miracle Twins	Margaret Barker

0614 GEN STD LP